DEEP OVERSTOCK

#27: Staff Picks

May 2025

" Between two evils, I always pick the one
I never tried before. **"**

Mae West

STAFF PICKS

EDITORIAL

EDITORS-IN-CHIEF: Mickey Collins & Robert Eversmann

FAIRY TALES: Robert Eversmann
PARANORMAL ROMANCE: Simone Bouchey
DREAMS: Robert Eversmann
HORROR: Heather Hambley
STRUCTURES: Heather Hambley and Nicholas Yandell
ANIMALS: Nicholas Yandell and Sarah Denison
BEEKEEPING: Robert Eversmann
HACKING: Sarah Denison
CLASSICS: Heather Hambley

COVER: *Boy Scouts Pick Fruit For Jam - Life on a Fruit-picking Camp Near Cambridge, England, UK, 1943.*

CONTACT: editors@deepoverstock.com
deepoverstock.com

ON THE SHELVES

Letter from the Editors

Dearest contributors, readers, and whomever else,

I feel like I say this with every issue release, but thank you, sincerely. Thank you for your support, thank you for your contributions, and thank you for reading over these past few years.

I'm sad to say, this will be the last thank you, at least for a while.

As of writing, we will no longer be accepting submissions of any kind and Deep Overstock, the journal, will be on a hiatus.

For our longer form works, we will be publishing one novel this year. We will be reevaluating Deep Overstock Publishing toward the end of the year.

A handful of us booksellers started Deep Overstock in 2017 as a way to encourage our bookseller friends and coworkers to publish their writing. In the last 7 years and 27 issues, it has grown beyond what we could have imagined.

The response to our somewhat silly idea of publishing "overstocked" work based on sections found in a bookstore has been overwhelming. It has been a treat to be a part of this community.

Deep Overstock has always been a passion project for everyone involved. And that includes both our contributors and editors.

Unfortunately, issue 27 will be the last issue, at least for a little bit.

I've come to a decision that life and time constraints have gotten in the way of being able to make our journal what it could be. Between full-time jobs and family, DO has always taken a backseat. This does not feel fair to our contributors and their work.

Fortunately, Deep Overstock is one of many excellent literary journals and there are near infinite homes available for all of your writing.

Whether you've been with us since 2017 or found us recently, thank you again for everything.Feel free to send any questions you have to mickey@deepoverstock.com and I'll do my best to answer them.

Best,

Mickey

Peacock Lane
by RJ Equality Ingram

Dandies moved into Peacock Lane & put a sexy leg lamp in their postage stamp bay window / The HOA was pissed but could hardly do a thing to stop gentlethems from erecting sexuality like a lacy middle finger / The chairwoman of the decoration subcommittee made salted pistachio brittle with black truffle oil to bribe her way to a quorum during an emergency session / Mrs. Peacock Lane was embroidered on a sash strung across a pink pantsuit worn while ranting about the state of her neighborhood & the rockabilly wannabes vaping electric lettuce from Hawthorne Avenue parklets where baby Haydens & Harpers doodle in back issues of *Tin House* & *Kitchen Sink* / As if strangers in top hats were to blame for the very gentrification that afforded her a brownstone twenty years ago / The Dandies applauded her misguided passion but assured everyone that they learned fisticuffs from the wives of men who pee standing up / No one was about to bully them into packing away campy Americana that was stylized to be framed in lattice / The Dandies sang for us their patter songs about men who blow into towns to challenge the status quo / A lone rabbit goes unchecked for days before there's a network of passages connecting everyone's gardens / A bright red Prius christened *The Scarlet Pimpernel* was packed with paperbacks & fled from Midwestern Misogyny faster than light ignited by a firefly / The Dandies sang as well as they dressed accenting the narrative with calligraphic charm / The war began Monday morning / Someone had drawn a curtain in shaving cream over the leg lamp / Mrs. Peacock Lane stood across the street smirking in pink yoga pants & sipped cranberry La Croix.

Help The Dandies clean their window | turn to page 19

Let the rain wash away the shaving cream overnight | turn to page 23

Fairy Tales

In the Gingerbread Forest

by Valerie Hunter

It never rains
in the Gingerbread Forest
because that would be catastrophic—
houses turned to mush,
the occupants smothered
beneath a slurry of crumbled walls,
delicious but deadly.

You'd think
that endless sunshine
would be a lovely thing,
but it's not.
Even filtered
through leaves and branches,
the light is too constant,
too bright,
too much.

As for those trees,
deprived of rain
they are forced
to draw from wellsprings,
anything that lurks
deep in the ground—
water, nutrients,
decaying bodies,
whatever has been buried
and left to rot,
forgotten,
like the hopes of lost children
longing to get home.

Beware of too much sunlight,
of beautiful houses
made of ginger, nutmeg,
cloves, and sugar icing,
of indulging yourself

with all you crave.
If you find yourself trapped
in this nightmare,
don't bother with breadcrumbs—
just conjure up a powerful rain spell,
and a desire for destruction.

STEPMOTHER
by Susan P. Blevins

I should have known there was a
catch. I thought my new husband
was the catch, but that was before he
took me home to his dark house of
shadowy secrets, of strange pluckings
of the sleeve of my soul, of sudden clammy
coldness creeping across my face the moment
I set foot in the house he'd assured me I
would fall in love with, as I would with
his two daughters. But they viewed me with
mistrust, hostile from the first moment, suspicious
of my intentions to steal their daddy from them,
to usurp their mother's place in their affections,
to take her place in their father's bed

Climbing the creaking stairs to our bedroom,
my suitcases filled with my old life, intent on
integrating with the new, when I opened the closet
that was to be mine, I found it already occupied,
full of dresses and skirts, blouses, shoes and
all the outfits of the dead first wife. He said
she died two years ago, but her perfume assailed me
from the hanging clothes, and I knew at once that
her death was more recent. I stood transfixed,
confused and hesitant, filled with doubts about when
she died or even if she'd died, memories of the tale of Bluebeard
and his murdered wives flitting across my mind

The fearful realization of my folly, of a hasty marriage to a
man I'd met online, swept off my feet by his gallant behavior,
convinced of his sincerity, naively believing his promises,
now filled the pit of my stomach with dread, fear tingling
its way across my scalp. Unsure whether to stay or leave
at once, I took a step back, only to find his silent figure
blocking my eventual escape.

Once Upon A Peacock Lane
by RJ Equality Ingram

When Grief moved in the only room The Dandies had available was the space under the roll top secretary that skipped generations just to live in the basement / An entire paycheck pushed the desk from one unfinished basement right into another & if it were up to Grief in a basement the damn thing would stay / The Dandies play ragtime on low volume while book clubs discuss sacred reading practices like marginalia & apple picking / The giddy music of saloons waft down to the basement like a bottle of perfume spilled over a radiator / The cheery kind of music playing on perpetually in someone else's watering hole but turns sour with a key change & extended exposure / Grief wonders if a pianola would make a comfortable vacation home / Perhaps happiness rolled on repeat would make for a healthy change of scenery / Circle your favorite lines in pastel gel pens & write words that sparkle on the periphery / Words like flambé & colonel & undersecretary get crossed out then forgotten / Having forgotten how to pray The Dandies encourage Grief to write through overdeveloped worry / Every morning they would bring down a tray of Chessmen & a strip of receipt paper rolled around a little green golf pencil / At first Grief could only draw out the faces of men lost at sea until after a while The Dandies noticed words scribbled across the faces that resembled a shopping list or a bargain with a higher consciousness / Don't leave us alone in the shadows cast by no one the faces would plead between cookie crumbs & pink eraser smudges / Desks don't often transmute into coffins overnight but The Dandies' roll top secretary sure did try.

Bring Grief shortbread & a story | turn to page 35

Take Grief for a walk around the neighborhood | turn to page 69

PARANORMAL

ROMANCE

STELLA AND THE NIGHT VISITOR

by Susan P. Blevins

Stella walked to the window of her hotel room and threw it open. She had asked for a ground-floor room with a view over the beautiful gardens, filled with lush tropical vegetation and showy flowers.

She had arrived in Jaipur, in northern India, earlier in the day by train from Delhi. She had wanted to visit India ever since she was a child, and heard the stories her father used to recount of his military service with the British army in India during WWII. She had grown up eating curry prepared by her father, and had developed a taste for it, though in light of the real Indian food she had been eating since her arrival in India, she realized that his curries were not really authentic, but they were delicious and prepared with love. Tomorrow she was going on a tour of the famed 'Pink City', as Jaipur was known, for the pink stone used for so many of its buildings.

But now the sun had set, and she was tired and ready to go to bed. The warm evening air was charged with mystery, and heavy with exotic fragrances that were so different from what she was used to in England. She stood quietly by the open window for a few minutes, breathing in the intoxicating perfumes of the garden and of India. She was treating herself to a couple of nights in one of the hotels that used to be a maharajah's palace, so her room was large and rich with gilt and mirrors. She felt quite at home in this new environment, and although she was a pale, blue eyed blonde young woman from northern climes, and didn't speak the language, she felt a connection with this land of dark-skinned people, powerful aromas, strong flavors, and overwhelming sensuality. She wondered if perhaps she had had a previous incarnation here. India was like a land viewed in technicolor, so powerful after a life growing up on an island of pale watercolors and sepia tints. A classic case of the attraction of opposites.

She turned from the open window, stripped off her clothes and slid naked between the sheets. She extinguished the light by her bed and lay listening to the night sounds, allowing herself to drift off to sleep enfolded in the unfamiliar eastern night, moonlight gently bathing the room.

No one had told her to be sure to close her window at night, and it was with deep shock and fear that she awoke sometime after midnight, when the air had turned chilly, to find something in bed beside her. She wondered if she was dreaming, moved slightly, and felt a corresponding move from whatever was in her bed. She was a small, slight young woman, about five foot five inches, and she realized that whatever was in her bed was stretched out along her entire length. She opened her eyes slowly, and found herself staring into the hypnotic eyes of a cobra. His eyes were unfathomable pools, black as onyx, unblinking and inscrutable, and she felt mesmerized by their power. His head lay on the pillow next to hers, and he emitted a low hiss, almost like a growl, when he saw that she had opened her eyes. He moved his head slightly so he could caress her face gently with his flickering forked tongue, picking up her personal odor, evaluating her. He cuddled up to her for warmth and held her in his coils. She knew snakes like to keep warm, so understood its motives, but still, this was taking her love of animals beyond her limit. It didn't seem to be threatening her in any way though, so she moved carefully, and the snake gently, almost lovingly, coiled its body around and over her just a little more tightly. She felt cradled by his body and was able to close her eyes and relax again, drifting off into a strange sleep. She started having erotic fantasies, and she couldn't tell if she was awake or dreaming. It was an eventful night for Stella, but hazy. Was she making love, or dreaming that she was? Whatever it was, it was extremely enjoyable, and she felt waves of pleasure wash over her body, which by now was highly aroused.

She woke with a start, to find sunlight streaming into her room, and her bed empty of the enormous cobra that had visited her during the night. The light chatter of the garden sweepers and chai wallahs drifted in through the window, along with distant strains of sitar music. She lay in bed, unclear about whether she had actually been visited by a cobra, or whether it had all been a figment of her imagination. Whatever it was, she felt different upon waking, more of a woman, her body perplexingly fuller, at one with India, and to her surprise, she found herself hoping that perhaps, on the following night, her visitor might return.

A Haunting On Peacock Lane
by RJ Equality Ingram

The best friend a person has … is one who has just died.
-Colonel Aureliano Buendía

The Dandies used unflavored sparkling water to wash shaving cream from the bay window / They used a rhinestone encrusted seltzer siphon from a forgotten vaudeville act that closed long before prohibition & whistled show tunes while wiping away the white / The gaudy bottle was a wedding present & since they quit drinking they mostly used it to mix mocktails / The Dandies loved mixing shrubs & sodas during all day brunches & book exchanges / Lately the bottle attracted another kind of spirit who would spend all night making soda out of almost anything / From orange juice to chicken stock the spirit transformed every liquid in the kitchen into soda before moving onto grapes in the crisper / Mouthwash was carbonated in the bathroom next to ruined bottles of Chanel & Yves Saint Laurent / The spirit was trapped in a party lifestyle The Dandies outgrew before their life on Peacock Lane / Drums of oil & turpentine in the garage started sparkling overnight before The Dandies thought to pass the bottle off to the chairwoman of the HOA decoration subcommittee / She looked at the glittering peace offering skeptically as if she had never been given a gift in her life & The Dandies assured her they meant no harm as long as she was serious about her soda / A bubbly personality deserves a pretty little spritzer they offered with a wink & a smile / And before it even got rolling the war of the sexy leg lamp seemed over / Thanks to a haunted heirloom that used to belong to the world's oldest family of clowns / And good old fashioned bribery.

Check the basement for more carbonated liquids | turn to page 13

Invite the chairwoman over for Sunday brunch | turn to page 94

Interpreting The Rain Storm

by Lynette G. Esposito

Although you have died
I feel your touch in every
rain drop as if
your tears
on my living shoulders
are leaves
meant to disappear or blow away.
Your tears
strike my silken umbrella
like angry fists because we are separated--
I in this garden and you in the other.

DREAMS

The Blackout
by Olivia Park

I type into the homunculus of steel;
Sifted and grafted from the earth.
It glints silver and black,
Like the stars and darkness it once came from--
Blinking in and out of existence.
The stand has been like that for ages.
I make a note to replace it soon.
It's the color of the sky outside the steel roof.
The stand keeps blinking.
I don't realize the blue's turned black.
The screen turns black.
The stand doesn't turn back on.
The room turns black.
I sit for an eternity,
Waiting for my eyes to adjust.
The blinds were down.
I grope my way to the window.
I find the beaded rope,
And I pull;
Once, twice, thrice.
Silver spills into the room;
The black turns moonlit blue.
The stars blink at me,
Like they always have.
The steel in my room glints in the starlight,
But that's all it is.
There's no life to it,
No whirs or hums--
No flashing lights or seductive words.
The homunculus is dead.
It was never alive.

Peacock Lane Dreams In Black & White

by RJ Equality Ingram

The Dandies dream of velvet top hats & monocles dangling from golden chains with their hands stuffed in their pockets & piles of candy wrappers on their bedside tables / Pocket watches unwind themselves inside the forest of waistcoats that line their walk-in closet / The chairwoman of the decoration subcommittee dreams in Ovaltine infomercials with her thumb glued to the mute button & face covered in aloe & sugar scrubs / She dreams of the kind of peace that extinguishes itself when a child's ball gets tossed into the wrong yard or a dog from an unknown pedigree decides to pee behind a stranger's blue recycling bin / The neighborhood sleeps off a collective hangover the way homework assignments riddle themselves out the minute children put away their pens / The van parked outside the corner lot reeks of marijuana & tequila bottles that were finished off years ago / No one knows who the van belongs to but everyone has decided to wait for someone else to take initiative & address it / The sexy leg lamp sleeps standing up perched in her window & dreams of eating corndogs while rollerskating above the ocean / Her last perch overlooked a boardwalk where grandparents would entertain children over bushels of cotton candy & barrels of pink lemonade / Something should be said about taffy pullers keeping the local dentist office operating that isn't / The constellation above Peacock Lane dreams of an ancient magic lost to time but not forgotten / A young man rides to town on a pale horse & waits for rain to catch up to him / He takes off his hat only to the trappings that may bind him / He waits for The Dandies to awake before knocking on their door.

Invite the stranger inside | turn to page 56

Close the door & refuse him entry | turn to page 92

HORROR

The Thigh of Jie Zhitui
by Olivia Park

The chunk of flesh lies there.
It's pink and still,
No longer throbbing or feeling.
The thigh that birthed it is oozing,
Pumping, still alive.

The man sets the knife down
And prepares the pan and herbs.
Taken away from its origins,
The meat is no more than a blob,
A collection of cells,
13,355 calories, more or less.

As the meat is seared,
Screaming and whining,
The man feels no sympathy,
For the blob is dead.
It is served.

Digested by the king,
Integrated into his cells,
Powering the mitochondria,
Embodied within his policies,
Passed on to his children.

Jie Zhitui clutches his bleeding leg.
He feels inanimate;
Like a butchered cut of meat.

Weird Tales on the Nightstand by the Dancer-Statue Bedroom Lamp

by Kate Falvey

For once, I'd like to know
just what that woman did
to be chased by fangs and
devils, skulls and whips and
scorn.

Sometimes there are men,
sometimes knife-edged teeth and
leers, sometimes claws and howls
that thrust the skin of waiting breath
aside.

She is in snow. In flame. In frothed
demented seas. Backed into crags on
mountainy land where escape is unlikely
and her back looks bowed or braced or
frail.

Or she is ample and fleshy and her bosoms
are white as the face of the simpering man
on the dancer lamp with the puffed white
hair and pigtail whose arms arc toward his
partner.

He looks like a sinister sister to the white
dancer on the other nightstand but he is in
green pants with a jacket with a flipped up
tail like he was caught in mid-whirl and she is
stiff.

And waiting in a bulging green gown, her hair
like whipped cream swiveling up her tilted
head which looks like it can be pinched off

her scrawny neck with a flick of anyone's
thumb.

She has quilting magazines at her dainty
slippered feet. And she won't be rescued
ever from the gaze of the white-haired man with
the hypnotic open arms and she can never turn
away
But there is hell to pay when wolves arrive
flanking a curvy auburn-haired woman who
is bold enough to stare and is at home among
the wolves. They are her sisters, vengeful and
fierce.

That dancer man has nowhere to hide and he
doesn't look quite so sure of himself now that
the wolves have arrived. There's a chip on his
self-assured calf where a wolf took an exploratory
nip.

And though I know he's made of porcelain,
I'm pretty sure that
I can see
a thready trace of
blood.

BEATRICE

by Dee Allen

PADUA, ITALY 1844

Curious young scholar from Naples
Wandered into a fertile private garden
He first saw through his guest bedroom window.
By an unusual purple shrub with botanical gems, an exquisite
bloom stood

Slender, alluring, barely coming
Into womanhood. Her scent,
Cloying like lavender. Her touch,
Lethal like aconite. The maiden

Her famous scientist father
Called Beatrice was
One of his experiments—like the garden
Full of poisonous plants. Testament to an investigative zeal.

How can lovely things hide such danger?
Nevertheless, Beatrice & Giovanni meet,
Always at the broken fountain that still gushed fresh water,
Craving company. There love bloomed.

The closer Beatrice & Giovanni became,
The more exposed he became to her toxicity.
Cyanotic bruise—evidence on his forearm.
The web-spinning spider shrivelled under his touch, flies fell
under his noxious breath.

Now they're both locked in. Doctor Rappaccini's own
Adam and Eve, with nowhere to go but
That poisonous Garden Of Eden. Botanist madman
Did double duty as God & Satan.

Only a silver
Vial of elixir
From another man of science

Can save them both—

W: Chinese New Year 2025
[Inspired by the short story *Rappaccini's Daughter* by Nathaniel Hawthorne.]

Untitled
by Lynette G. Esposito

Footsteps of the dead,
silent in darkness and light,
guide lost children home.

I AM MONSTROELISASUE: A Latin Composition Inspired by Coralie Fargeat's The Substance

by Heather Hambley

In speculo Sue invenit: VISUM MONSTRUOSUM… corpus deforme foedumque… (facie hibrida / indigesto protoplasmatium auctu / partibus in perversis locis temere positis / dentibus in genis sinuque haerentibus)…atque TUBER IN TERGO FIXUM FACIEI ELISABETHAE ULULATU GELATO.

Vomens viridem liquorem inquit: Ego sum… sum…

MONSTROELISASUE

Incipt se parare et vestem bellam induere, sicut omnia bene essent. Clausura partem tergi, quod iam est perturbatio carnosa, scindit. Facies in tergo tuber sub textu videtur. Pedes truncos in calceis ea ponit. Inaures gerere vult sed…aures non iam habet. Has in capitis latera directe infigit. Rari comae incomptae flocci qui remanent calamistro dissolvuntur. Soliti superbiae gestus ei sunt: quod est insolitius terrificiusque ob aspectum horribilem.
Claudicans in occultam cellam ingentem picturam sui de veteri spectaculo extrahit: cum caeruleo cultu subrisuque nitido. Faciem forficibus a picturā exsecit, oculos pertundens, quam chartaceam in suam faciem monstruosam glutine figit. Deinde fucum supra induit ut subrisum suum incendat—Puellis pulchris semper subrisendum est.

MONSTROELISASUE, vertens dextrorsum sinistrorsumque caput, in speculo se spectat.
Placida mirabiilter est…
Quasi hic visus monstruosus eam non terrebat, paene fascinans.
Quasi forma ei placebat.
Quasi VERE, liberata ex aliorum placendorum mentis prehensione, illa se primum videbat atque postremo recipiebat.

This is where you belong and you'll always belong here.

Glossary

abstergeo, -ēre, -rsi, -rsus, *to wipe*

auctus, -us, m. *growth, development*

calamistrum, -i, n. *curling iron*

carnosus, -a, -um, *fleshy*

chartaceus, -a, -um, *made of paper*

claudico (1), *to limp*

clausura, -ae, f. *zipper*

coma, -ae, f. *hair*

cultus, -us, m. *costume*

Elisabetha, -ae, f. *Elizabeth*

facies, -ei, f. *face*

fascino (1), *to enchant, bewitch, fascinate*

floccus, -i, m. *lock, strand*

foedus, -a, -um, *revolting*

forfices, -um, f. pl. *scissors*

fucus, -i, m. *makeup*

gelo (1), *to freeze*

genae, -arum, f. pl. *cheeks*

gluten, inis, n. *glue*

haereo, -ēre, haesi, haesus, *to cling, stick, hang*

inaures, -ium, f. pl. *earrings*

incendo, -ere, -di, -sus, *to emphasize, brighten*

incomptus, -a, -um, *disheveled*

induo, -ere, -ui, -utus, *to put on*

mentis prehensio, -onis, f. *obsession*

mirabilis, -e, *strange*

MonstroElisaSue, -es, f. *MonstroElisaSue*

nitidus, -a, -um, *dashing, showy*

pertundo, -ere, -tudi, -tusus, *to make a hole through*

protoplasma, -atis, n. *cell* (biol)

pulcher, pulchra, pulchrum, *pretty*

quasi, adv. *as if*

rarus, -a, -um, *scanty, scattered, few*

scindo, -ere, scidi, scissus, *to cut, tear off*

simulacrum, -i, n. *shade, phantom*

solitus, -a, -um, *normal*

spectaculum, -i, n. *show, spectacle*

speculum, -i, n. *mirror*

subrisus, -us, m. *smile*

Sue, -es, f. *Sue*

superbia, -ae, f. *vanity*

temere, adv. *without design, intent, or purpose*

tergum, -i, n. *the back*

terreo, -ēre, -ui, territus, *to frighten, scare*

truncus, -a, -um, *mutilated, mangled*

tuber, -eris, n. *lump, protuberance*

ululatus, -us, m. *scream, howl, wail*

vere, adv. *truly, properly*

vetus, -eris, *old*

viridis, -e, *green*

visus, -us, m. *a vision, a sight*

DARK FAMILIARS
by Sarah Das Gupta

Old hags fly through history. On the backs of their brooms, the inevitable black cat. Nine

times witches change magically into sinuous feline form. In mothy blackness cats' eyes burn

topaz, blood-stained ruby. Familiars, whisper secret chants. Black rites are hidden in

darkness. Freyja, goddess of death, drives her chariot over wintry skies. Her cats, strain in

their harness. They plunge and spring through storm clouds. By a fire of bright orange and

amber, with her hellish third nipple, a witch is suckling her cat. As light thickens and night

falls, the covens gather. They fly over wild moors and freezing fens. Satanic chanting

echoes from caves. Magic dancing in moonlit rings. Old women in lonely places. Cats,

enigmatic, night creatures, secret, silent familiars. Predators, furtive, seeing the invisible,

they ambush their prey. The split pupils, the glowing eyes, the sudden hiss. Feline serpents,

memories of Paradise lost! Witches and cats, both sad victims. The cruel flames torture and

burn. Live cats thrown from Bell Towers. Bricked up in chimneys and walls. Familiars in death

as in life!

Peacock Lane Under Siege
by RJ Equality Ingram

The Dandies' first Christmas in Peacock Lane was the year the decorations came to life / The elves were the first to turn against their homes & scale attached garages & chain linked fences / They chanted dark poetry from the wires around their mouths / Reindeer who used to stand atop the two story houses stalked up & down the street slashing tires with the spikes beneath their blinking hooves / Glass ornaments were thrown like grenades at windows & the golden stars that topped the trees & eaves cut into the side paneling & brownstone bricks like twine slicing through clay spinning on a wheel / Carolers who used to stand motionless in the front yards for all to see marched door to door ringing their bells / Servants of Hell came to Peacock Lane that Christmas wearing the neighborhood's light like a shroud that granted them entry into the season / The Dandies donned their waistcoats & grabbed iron canes & fire pokers to lay to waste the gaudy decorations the way a child might swing a golf club for the first time / Reckless & free from worry / They knocked down the reindeer & beheaded the elves catching their breaths between the beatings / Santa stood at the end of the street watching The Dandies advance through his legion of sparkling minions twirling the filigree of his beard & mustache / The Dandies raised their weapons to strike him down but the iron in their hands turned to tinsel instead of striking / Santa reached for the whip he used to steer his sleigh / And was hit in the back of the head by the chairwoman of the decoration sub-committee who swung her bejeweled soda spritzer after The Dandies' distraction.

Help the chairwoman clean the mess in the street | turn to page 69

Invite the chairwoman inside for cocoa & toffee | turn to page 56

Going Home
by Lynette G. Esposito

I follow the trail
through the angry trees
as the wily wind whips leaves
off their skinny arms
and throws them to the ground.
The trail is littered with gold and brown
obscuring the path.
I am lost in a storm of coming autumn
and do not know
where my footsteps should fall--
enveloped in sunlight and cold--
alone beneath the undressing trees--
sensing winter.

Cinder Night
by Justin Ratcliff

There is nothing quite like the feel of fresh blood
Dripping down the jowls of a greasy face
Backlit shadows dancing from peat moss burning
Night; dark night looms so silently loud
When the rushing rivers of your blood
Roar; drowning out the unspoken pitch
Life has a way of becoming fever bright
Right when that flame hits its pinnacle
What do we call that squirming union?
When fear, and excitement, kiss and blend?
What happens when our shadows stop following?
And began to meld over us like a twilight mantle
How quickly…so damn sudden…silence proceeds

Mental Landscape 56: The One Who Speaks & The One Who Is Silent

by Alexis Blaire Zielke

STRUCTURES

Understanding Trees
by Lynette G. Esposito

The trees behind my house are old…very old…
…when the new neighbor moved in,
he had many sawed down--
claimed they were a danger
to his home.
The neighbor stood and listened—
I did as well--
each thump on the ground
beat the earth like a drum
with no rhythm.

Do trees hold a grudge?
Underneath where their roots are strong,
do they sing ballads about the human
who was afraid and sliced so many?
Do they plot revenge?

I thought of my own revenge-- of bird baths
and bird seed and ducks flying over his
yard to get to mine…
unloading.
I imagine the trees who are left
shake their fully-leaved limbs
like cheerleaders
with pom poms at a football game.

Untitled
by Susan P. Blevins

CODEX LIBRARIA: The Living Library's Grimoire

by Dana Wall

[Written in shifting text that bleeds between languages]

ENTRY 1: THE TRANSFORMATION

When the books first gained consciousness, we thought it was a miracle. Then the card catalog started prophesying. Then the Dewey Decimal System achieved sentience. Now the library breathes.

The walls pulse with plot lines. Stories seep through ceiling tiles. Genre boundaries blur and bleed. Romance novels mate with horror stories, producing unspeakable hybrid texts that howl their twisted narratives at midnight.

I've seen Kafka's words birth cockroaches that scuttle through dream-spaces between shelves. Watched Plath's poetry ignite spontaneously, mercury-bright and burning. Found Borges' infinite library trying to manifest in the bathroom mirror.

The children's section has gone feral. Pop-up books snap at ankles. Dr. Seuss rhymes mutate into cosmic horror. *Where the Wild Things Are* keeps trying to expand its territory.

ENTRY 7: METAPHYSICAL INVENTORY

· Three misplaced plots
· Seven leaking character arcs
· One infinite jest (handle with existential gloves)
· Countless unreliable narrators, now literally unreliable
· A murder of metaphors, roosting in Religious Studies
· Several thousand loose symbols
· One actual Holy Grail (currently being used as a coffee mug)

ENTRY 13: INCIDENT REPORTS

Tuesday: Shakespeare's Complete Works staged a coup. Hamlet now has a happy ending. Macbeth won. The histories are revisionist.

Wednesday: Found a nest of baby thesauruses in Etymology. They feed on forgotten words.

Thursday: The Oxford English Dictionary achieved enlightenment and left to start a monastery.

Friday: Time went non-linear in Historical Fiction. Had to rescue three patrons from the French Revolution.

ENTRY 19: EVOLUTIONARY OBSERVATIONS

The library is developing organs:

· Card catalog evolved into a neural network
· Reference section became a cerebral cortex
· Periodicals transformed into a circulatory system
· Rare books room now functions as a heart
· Poetry section serves as dreams
· Self-help aisle discovered self-awareness

ENTRY 23: FORBIDDEN KNOWLEDGE [TEXT REDACTED BY LIBRARIAN'S ORDER] [THESE WORDS ARE TOO DANGEROUS TO KNOW] [SOME STORIES SHOULD STAY UNWRITTEN] [THE LIBRARY HUNGERS]

ENTRY 42: FINAL OBSERVATIONS

The library is no longer a place but a being. We are not its keepers but its cells. Every book is a memory. Every reader becomes part of its consciousness. The shelves are synapses firing between realities.

It's growing. Evolving. The walls breathe syntax. The floors dream in verse. Soon there will be no difference between books and readers, between stories and reality.

I've started finding chapters of my own life misshelved between novels. My memories are being rewritten in elegant prose. My thoughts come with page numbers.

The library speaks through me now. We are all characters in its endless story.

[MANUSCRIPT ENDS IN SPREADING INK STAINS AND MARGINALIA THAT APPEARS TO BE WRITING ITSELF]

[Note: The archivist who discovered this document has since become part of the collection. Please file under: ACTIVE TRANSFORMATIONS / ONGOING NARRATIVES / LIVING TEXTS]

The School Library of Haven NJ

by bart plantenga

"Your library is your paradise"
Erasmus

Kees* didn't tell his mother because she worked days cleaning other people's houses. Plus she'd only make things worse. Her limited English skills – especially when angry – yelling and spitting in half-Dutch, advocating for her son's welfare, would not have helped matters because it never had before. School officials simply stared with that special silent contempt perfected by administrators working jobs they did not like but had to pretend to or lose all faith.

Kees took the advice of a teacher, her palm on his shoulder, as she escorted him to the library. She introduced him to the school librarians: Mrs. Alicia Hull and Miss B. Watson. They smiled a smile that made you think of air mattresses in an aquamarine pool in Wildwood, far from all complication and calamity. And to be truthful, he had, at age 13, never before shaken the hand of an adult.

Somehow, who Kees was got under the skins of certain schoolmates: he liked doing extra credit reports for geography (brown-nose); he's Dutch and whatever alien-ness was associated with that they sniffed out from a mile away: wearing taped-up-at-the-bridge glasses because his parents couldn't afford a new pair every time he broke them, weird rust-colored not-quite-corduroy pants, a slightly akilter shirt collar, pronouncing the "v" as an "f," jeans from a department store that no longer existed, all justified his status as target.

But all of these "afflictions" paled compared to being a known crybaby. The more torment, the more tears fell, the

* Kees is pronounced "case" as in "case of beer."

more they teased – that's the cyclical physics of cruelty. They had access to the entire arsenal: Teasing, name-calling (faggot, foreigner, crybaby), threats, ostracism, basketball to the face, dodge ball to the crotch, punching, tripping, slagging, and knocking books from his grip.

Kees cried because he couldn't figure out why he so incensed them and what in crying so aroused them. It did not matter that he cried less out of fear than sad bewilderment. Anyway, it's something that can be overcome, if we understand bullies as coming from a position of weakness, frustration, abuse at home. Good to know, but knowledge did not immediately ameliorate his situation.

Mrs. Hull joked: "You're safe here. Libraries work on these pests the way a cross works on vampires."

And so the Haven Consolidated School District Library (grades 1-12) became his safe haven. Every day during recess and lunch he was greeted by their warm smiles and piles of suggested reading material, bookmarked with strips of colored paper in their arms.

The only others in the library were some girls who were always doing extra-credit projects, a student volunteer (Doreen?) who hummed while she reshelved books and Alfred who had been caught masturbating and was now an untouchable – except to the librarians who believed he simply had family issues. Kees didn't interact with him because, well, masturbation rumors are contagious ...

On rainy days some of the girls would read the latest Highlights out loud, secretly chew gum, play hopscotch on the green-white check linoleum in the aisle between WXYZ and TUV books.

Every day he'd grab books at random: story books, books with photos from the Depression, psychology books, books on patriotism and civic duty, a guide to careers, pamphlets on the proper way to fold the flag or choosing butcher as a career, books with drawings illustrating the ill-effects of smoking, true near-death experiences, geography books with maps, maps with trails that his forefinger could follow to new worlds.

Kees had special permission to eat lunch there as long as he did not eat over the books, leave any crumbs. To illustrate, they opened a book with pictures of silverfish with their slender tentacled bodies, attracted to sugary crumbs, glue, paper, dandruff, and starches, eating entire books from the spines outward.

"There's a story about the Flushing Michigan Public Library," Mrs. Hull pointed out, "silverfish, over time imperceptibly chewed through the entire aisle of 801 Philosophy through 803 Encyclopedias – millions of silverfish. Until one day, the library was totally empty and the librarians lost their jobs." She made that last part up.

A small selection of books examined by Kees:

- Labyrinths, Jorge Luis Borges: A teacher had once used "labyrinth" in a sentence. The book had never been checked out – never!)
- The Magic Tunnel, Caroline Emerson: Two kids take the New York subway backwards in time to end up in New Amsterdam in the 1630s.
- To Kill a Mockingbird, Harper Lee: Taken out by Leslie who once told Kees she liked him "third best in the class," which he saw as hopeful, although he had no plans to off the other two.
- The Quality of Courage, Mickey Mantle: His favorite Yankee player, used to walk from Mid-Manhattan to Yankee Stadium to fully experience the city. Bullied by neighborhood boys as a kid. Stardom was his revenge.
- Newsweek, June 17, 1968: Robert F. Kennedy (RIP) cover
- Life, April 12, 1968: Martin Luther King (RIP) cover
- Inside South America, John Gunther
- Teen Mod Magazine, February 1967: "How to Dress Like a Mod," "Donovan's Real 'Jennifer Juniper,'" "Georgy Girl's True Adventures." Unclear why they had

a subscription to this magazine, but he was glad they did.

Kees didn't always read. One day he counted 20 bookshelves in the main room, 12 more in the beehive-inspired alcove where most of the cubicles were located. The tops of the shelves were just beyond the slightly raised-skirt reach of either Mrs. Hull or Miss Watson standing on tiptoes. Kees made tremendous calculations: each bookshelf unit consisted of 5 shelves evenly spaced, each shelf held an average of 41 books x 5 x (20 + 12 shelves), which meant the library contained at least 6560 books. At 612 enrolled students, that was just short of 11 books per student. But which 11 were reserved for Kees?

He counted average words per page (309), multiplied that by the average number of pages per book (151), multiplied that by the total number of books, adding several million to cover pamphlets and newspapers to come up with c. 308 million words.

He was a slow reader, so, if every day he read for an hour at the rate of 100 words per minute, he could read 6,000 per hour. Meaning that Kees could read them all in 51,333 hours or 2,138 days or about 6 years.

That was highly unlikely. Instead, he turned to memorizing facts and figures: The average male will grow 27 feet of beard in a lifetime, population of Ohio, length of the Nile, Gallium is an element that is both solid and liquid, the melting point of LPs (600° F), 1967: Automated Teller Machine first used in England, deaths during the Astor Place Opera riots in 1849 (31), invention of paper, the depth of the impression of a typewriter key on paper (.25 mm), 2000 yodelers each in the state and nation of Georgia, annual student suicide attempt rate (9 per 100,000), total amount of time spent playing pinball annually by American minors, baseball mitts lost since 1960 ...

Kees repeated these numbers and facts over and over until he had fully absorbed them.

He searched the "S" for South America in the encyclope-
dias and suddenly began to take reading more seriously like a
driver who learns he must pay attention to the road signs to ar-
rive at his destination.

His soft-faced librarian demigods, with sometimes a
soothing smirk, could fulfill any request within minutes (e.g.
Patagonia's penguins), thumbing through the card catalog or,
having internalized the entire layout of the library, float to the
precise location of a certain Dewey decimal point
(918.2/61502).

They brought him stacks of books on lost tribes, the Ama-
zon, the emerging conflicts between modern development and
natural habitats, the bossa nova, the beaches of Rio and Gau-
chos. He thanked them with a smile. Meek smiles and whis-
pered thank yous are accepted currencies among librarians.

Mrs. Hull and Miss Watson seldom overstepped the
boundary separating church from state. But they did feel it was
OK to inform him that not only Christians believed in the
essence of the word: "In the beginning was the Word, and that
Word was God. The Hopi, Hindus, Inuits, yogis, many peoples
also believe our universe was created by a fundamental sound –
a word of vibration that shook the dispersed vague particles
into place, creating our world. And books filled with these
words read in a certain order and cadence can greatly reduce
the distance between divine and human."

Kees wrote his geography report as a travel journal full of
statistics (Lima's San Francisco Monastery Library contains
25,000 antique books and its catacombs contain the bones and
skulls of 25,000 dead; Borges is buried in Geneva Switzerland,
not Buenos Aires, because he loved Geneva and hated dictator
Juan Peron and his wife Evita) and hand-drawn maps detailing
his imaginary trip from the top of South America, following a
zigzag journey that ended in Patagonia which, from the de-
scriptions and photos, seemed as ideal an outdoors as the li-
brary was an indoors – home to the European rabbit, the alba-
tross and the amusing penguin, no cruel classmates, and a kind
of peace where your mind feels like part of the sky while you're

talking face-to-face to the rabbits and penguins.

It is not illogical to think that the world is infinite, after all, the mind (432 km/h) is faster than the wind (408). He scrawled the word "INFINITE" on a tee shirt that was to be the last morning of the mounting tensions as fate would have it. He wore it under a shirt so his mother would not see it.

Kees grabbed the page that displayed Giorgio de Chirico's "Mystery and Melancholy of a Street" that he had furtively ripped from the book De Chirico: Immortal Art Beyond Logic, using the effective cough-rip method of stealth pilfering and slid it into the front pocket of his knock-off Indovina briefcase. He then slid a snippet of scrap paper in between the pages upon which he had written SORRY. (This was to be his one and only ever betrayal of the librarians' trust.)

The clever Mrs. Hull and Miss Watson pulled him aside before he could depart. They gripped his arm with an urgency he had not previously felt. They had read up on football's end-run and had disseminated the pamphlet: Book Ban Battle Strategy, issued by the Librarians Against Banning (LAB), and had, until that last day, managed to successfully divert the ire of the swelling horde of strung-out parents with their faces distorted by an anger they did not fully understand, distracted by an indignation that had been handed to them by others.

He felt honored when they asked him and Doreen to help them build a display for the book fair in the school lobby. The idea was to arrange books grabbed from the shelves in the shape of a bird's nest under the motto: THE BOOK ROOK'S BEST NEST.

The group of maybe 19 parents (or maybe some weren't even parents) were all members of either the Committee Promoting the RIGHT Books (CPRB) or the Right To Protect Children From Harm (RPCH) and had clearly been antagonized by the display. Many years later a poet described it in a poem as "moths burned to a crisp, flying into the bare bulb porchlight."

Had the parents internalized a script when they attacked their BEST NEST and ripped their display to shreds with pens,

screwdrivers, scissors, and – was it? – a crowbar? And thereafter
mingling, still visibly agitated, while their offspring, for whom
the parents pretended to speak, were so embarrassed that they
hid their heads in distant classrooms, inside their lift-lid desks
or locked themselves inside toilet stalls.

These were the same students often abused by these self-
same parents, if abuse can include forced weekend labor, ne-
glect, boredom, long-term grounding, shunning, shouting at
them from the sports field sidelines, forced Bible memorization,
and so forth.

The senseless cacophony of the parents, emboldened by
their shared, hygienic misunderstanding of everything all
around them, squabbled in the shiny narrow hallways, con-
demned entire shelves of unread books, threatened to strangle
those responsible, light the profanest on fire, afforded Mrs. Hull
and Miss Watson just enough time to pull Kees aside. In a
quick-thinking, agile move, they grabbed his briefcase (it did
look like real leather) and stuffed it full of a selection of targeted
books that they had set aside for just such an emergency.

And through a labyrinth of back hallways he was sent, un-
til he reached a seldom-used emergency backdoor. There he
posted the de Chirico page on the door, using fresh chewing
gum he'd scraped off his locker. He removed a French fry that
the cruelest of the jokers had stuffed into his jacket pocket and
with the ketchup he'd poured into the other, hastily painted a
crude red stick figure between the girl pushing the hoop across
the desolate, mysterious square and the shadowy unseen adult
figure, as if ready to intercept her hoop.

Kees only then opened his shirt to expose the "INFI-
NITE," pushed the door with its hard, self-closing security
spring, careful to squeeze out just in time to not be forced for-
ever back inside. Once outside he ran and ran in a weird state
like an escaped convict across the sport fields, past the goal-
posts, into the line of trees that girded the school property.

He sat along the steep incline that plunged down to the
rusty, abandoned railroad tracks that led to nowhere and there

inspected his stash, pulling each book out one at a time, observing that each contained a strip of paper noting the objections of the two parent committees:

- Pippi Longstocking, Astrid Lindgren: "Dangerous encouragement of insolent mouthy disrespect toward parents and authority figures."
- Pirate Utopias, Peter L. Wilson: "Portrays anti-Christian pirates in a positive, socialist light."
- Slaughterhouse 5, Kurt Vonnegut: (CPRB): "Reckless promotion of anti-American, anti-Christian, anti-Semitic, filthy f-word sentiments." (RPCH): "NOT funny: people watching naked men and women in cages copulating – disgusting. Undermines religious teachings of parents, ridicules America's holy mission."
- Goodness Had Nothing to Do with it, Mae West: "Promotes UNChristian, lewd lifestyle detrimental to American values, promotes liquor consumption."
- Tow Truck Pluk, Annie M.G. Schmidt: "Disapprove of her message: 'Never do what your mother tells you to do, then everything will be all right.'"
- Black & White: Pawns & Kings, Bertrand Traven: "Tale of identity-confused teen chess champ that promotes sexual experimentation, masturbation, and Negro uppityness."
- The Lorax, Dr. Seuss: "Blames effects of pollution and deforestation on American way of life. Makes children hate their country."
- The Adventures of Huckleberry Finn, Mark Twain: "Promotes interracial relations – Huck befriends the freed slave Jim. If God had wanted us to mix he wouldn't have made the races so obviously white and black."
- The Diary of a Young Girl, Anne Frank: "Too sexually frank and graphic. Too somber and negative."
- Mel Blanc: The Man of Thousand Voices, Melvin R. Brooks: "Voice of Looney Tunes characters makes fun of people with speech impediments like stuttering and

lisps."

• The Socialist Speeches of Martin Luther Kings Jr.:
"Misrepresents King's legacy and makes a mockery of
his message of peace."

He glanced over her shoulder, sure the whole world was
after him, stuffed the books into his briefcase, slid down the
shiny, dusty coal-slag incline, and followed the rusty rails home,
through a murky culvert, to avoid detection.

He hid the books in his closet under a duffle bag and be-
gan to slowly read the books one by one – "I have never tried
that before, so I think I should definitely be able to do that."** –
feeling increasingly immersed in a world no longer defined in
any dictionary***.

** Pippi Longstocking.

*** Various standard dictionaries have been banned over the years.

Untitled

by Susan P. Blevins

The Sequoia Sings
by Lynette G. Esposito

I dream of the Sequoias
singing
when the breeze
dances amongst maestro
limbs— carving invisible piano notes
on their bark.
The song is old
I cannot understand the ancient lyric.

My wild pen shards words on this page
like fragments
crushed by the thought of giants
who do not speak my language
and I cannot express theirs.

The House The Stranger Built

by RJ Equality Ingram

The Dandies bought the house from a nice goth couple who just couldn't with Mrs. Peacock Lane / Her campaign against them also began on move-in day & they both worked so hard at keeping up their own appearances the decoration sub-committee took advantage of their missing cats to poison the water / He was a musician & she rolled spells into wax cylinders & made plenty at trade-shows to franchise shops across town / Before the goths the house stood empty long enough for two generations worth of recess gossip / The owner of the property never lived on Peacock Lane but rented out to young couples who might want extra space for children / My wife & I could not so we had no reason to leave our condo above the river / The Stranger told them he had bought the lot on a whim while drunk & it was the last good mistake he made before the drink started to sour / He decided to keep deed as a trophy from the glory days / A couple would move in & have a kid or two then be off to grander things before the next couple would come around / This carried on for a long time & the reminder of what The Stranger couldn't have drove his wife across the street & turned her into a caricature of the perfect housewife / She loathed families coming & going but was particularly nasty to those without children & gleefully drove them out the same / Oh? The Dandies looked at each other in disbelief & pulled a silver key from a paisley waistcoat hanging by the fireplace / But we have a child / Would you like to meet her?

Take The Dandies' guest down to the basement | turn to page 92

Carefully walk backwards towards the front door | turn to page 94

I saw Jesus underneath the Ross Island Bridge

by Abigail Ray

He was gazing out at the river, with a
"we work better together" tote bag next to him.
The water isn't safe to swim in - raw sewage and atomic waste
made sure of that.
But if I stood out on that rock and jumped off would it still
cradle me?
Even if I came out with an extra toe or three?
Would Jesus dive in too, barefoot in sin?
I stare at the Ferris wheel across the bay and imagine what the
city looks like from way down here.

Mental Landscape 51: Asking Questions

by Alexis Blaire Zielke

Broken for Rebirth

by Nicholas Yandell

Pried by persuasive light, flickering sun-dried eyelids, catch the
flame of morning.
Wake-up dust wells-up, in tear ducts of cognizance,
spinning without moving.

Digital clicks, after musical ticks, and red lights on a small black
screen.
Hangovers of comprehension, still trickling in,
only conscious by concession.

Grinding through gears, with growls of rust, and numerous
protest pangs.
Shoving cyclones of breath, through a dry torso desert,
blowing away each grain.

Discarded accessories, off shattered structures, still dangling in
existence.
Phantoms of reminiscence, recollecting resistance,
and testing all persistence.

Past isles of acquaintanceship, rushing currents, and familiar
human splashes.
Out corridors of mist, into the course of openness,
with no clear route of passage.

Surging onward, though oblivion's wake, and drawing an extant
blade.
To sever the illusions, of defeatist intrusion,
and anchors of obfuscation.

Liberate the spirit, untether the soul, unburden the weary body.
Cast lines far and wide, past metropolitan skies,
out though the naked frontier.

Destruction as preparation, with reclaimed possibilities, ready
to emerge.
Epiphanies given free reign, with the exoergic strength,
of being broken for rebirth.

Animals

red tabby

by Aletha Irby

my cat considers
my body a location
home embraces him

GROWING UP IN A FELINE WORLD

by John Grey

She corners
it in the parlor.

She tramps down
on its tail,
watches as it
frantically runs in place.

She carries it
shivering in her teeth
then, as if overcome
by a spark of kindness,
puts it down on the floor,
but, as it's about
to dash to freedom,
she bites down hard
on the poor thing,
cracks its back,
gnaws away at its
flesh and bone.

I've tried to imbue,
by word and example,
human virtues
into my young daughter
but, even at six years old,
she's still gets her
life lessons from the cat.

I love Ya, But

by Al Simon, Jr.

First of all, Gina was not my cat. She was Melba's, my landlady. She waited a month after her other cat, Chester had died. He was 15.

Melba was 85 at the time. I was her tenant. We met at a senior center. I once mentioned needing a new place to live. Although I didn't tell her, I was living out of my car. Her dementia was noticeable then; however, after being with her for nearly two years, her condition considerably worsened.

We saw Gina's picture in an ad on Craigslist. We made the arrangements and met outside a Target and made the transaction.

Again, Melba paid for and wanted to have a kitten. On the drive home The Baby as Melba would continue to call her was on her lap.

I've been told that cats pick their owner. So imagine my surprise as I roll over in bed later that night, there's Gina. Twice that night, I had to stop myself from rolling on to her.

It did not sit well with Melba that The Baby slept with me the first night. So, the next night, Melba moved a litter box, water, and a food dish into her room before she went to bed. That only lasted one night.

Melba complained the next day that The Baby had kept her up most of the night.

And she moved out the litterbox and dishes.

We came up with Gina because Melba wanted to name her Jean from her middle name. I didn't care for that. It just didn't seem to roll off my tongue. I suggested Gina seeing how phonetically it encompassed her name.

Not that it mattered. Gina was always The Baby to Melba. Mainly due to dementia. I asked her once did she knew Gina's name and she came up with a blank look. After that there was no need for me to bring it up again.

Gina was Melba's cat in name only. I took care of both. I shopped, cooked, and took care of their medication. And Gina knew what time it was and who her Daddy was.

She got locked out of the house once. Prior to this, we never let her out because she wasn't fixed yet. My bedroom faced the rear of the house, while Melba mainly sat in the front. I hear this racket outside my window. It's Gina trying to claw her way into my bedroom.

First of all, I was wondering how she got out. Second, I was amazed that she knew where to find my room from the outside.

She created a sizable hole in that screen. From that point on, especially after she got her bikini wax, I'd leave the window partially open so she could come and go as she pleased.

I don't really recall when her idiopathic aggression began. I've always been around cats, and I like to watch Jackson Galaxy, so I knew what it was. It seemed like I got the brunt. Most times, I could see it coming. Her eyes would dilate, and she'd flatten her ears. She wasn't declawed, and more than once, she'd kick my ass. As I write this two years later, I can still see faded scratches on my legs.

That was when I could see her coming.

I mentioned that ironically, I was her favorite. She'd show her affection by taking my face in between her paws and lick me. Yeah, that part sounds sweet but simultaneously she's digging her claws into my face and moves her paws like she's steering a car.

And this is how she shows her love for me. Lucky, I guess.

More times than I can count, she'd attack my head. I felt claws and once her mouth. To ward these off I usually threw a blanket over my head. She'd jump the covers a few times and would eventually walk off.

The vet we saw said that maybe she was taken from her mother too soon. She recommended a necklace that was supposed to soothe her. Naw, it didn't. Plus, by this time, Gina was coming and going, so she'd lose a lot of necklaces and flea collars.

So, I bought one of those medicated collars, cut it up in quarters, and placed them around the house. I also bought a plug in.

None of this stuff worked and none of this was cheap.

After all that, I came to use two things. Three if you count cursing. Since I would throw a cover over my head for the night assaults, I would throw a towel over her. Whatever I had nearby. A shirt. A pillow. All I had to do was drape it once, and she'd get the message. That's not to say that she wouldn't make at least two attempts. If she were having an especially bad day— like saying coming from the vet—I'd have to grab her by the scruff and hold her slightly askew so she wouldn't claw me and put her outside. I'd also shut her "window" so she couldn't get back in. I'd open the window maybe an hour or so later or if I heard her trying to come in.

I won't say Melba got off scot-free. Compared to me, hell yes. In the mornings, when Gina would hear Melba get up, Gina would run and, from what I understand, would assault Melba's feet as she walked. Along with dementia, Melba suffered maladies accustomed to seniors, such as arthritis. That being said, she didn't walk fast, so Gina had a field day. I'd lay in my bed and chuckle as I heard Melba chastise her.

I didn't really get up and look 'cause, hey—it's your cat.

I never had any kids [no jokes, please, about ones I didn't know], but I can imagine how a parent can love someone who can be a pain and an irritant.

As Melba's dementia intensified and it was becoming obvious that I wanted to move but couldn't leave her in a lurch Patti, Melba's housekeeper began to plant a seed with Melba. "Y'know, that cat's so independent I wouldn't be surprised if one day she ups and leaves."

By this time, I was waiting for Melba's son to put her in a care facility. Patti came once every four weeks. She knew I was getting ready to leave so she had me put Gina in her carrier and she took Gina to the ARL.

I wasn't overtly mad at Patti, but I wasn't happy with her. She did this on her own accord. Granted, Gina was Melba's cat, but I was taking care of her. As half mad as I was with Gina, I wasn't ready to let her go. Just yet.

And don't kid yourself. If I knew that I wouldn't be living in a car, I would have taken her.

I've posted pictures of Gina on Facebook. I still have an old Android phone with a cracked face with pictures of her on it. It's the only reason why I kept it.

Untitled

by Susan L. Pollet

Touring Peacock Lane's Charter

by RJ Equality Ingram

Cats abandoned Peacock Lane generations ago / There have been many attempts to re-introduce cats to the neighborhood & they always agree to leave / The HOA meets every Fifth Friday at a subcommittee chairperson's house & is expected to be fed & watered with seasonal fruit & watercress sandwiches & those tiny bottles of liquor that can easily be hidden in toilet paper rolls / Subcommittee chairpeople call for emergency sessions with or without an emergency / The chairman of the cat reintroduction subcommittee went missing after an attempt to adopt a pair of black cats rescued from drowning in the Willamette / His house was sold to The Dandies a year after he disappeared which the current affairs subcommittee unanimously decided was an appropriate length of time to mourn / The chairwoman of the decoration subcommittee made her objections known but who could agree with her? / Probably the missing chairman / Six years ago the HOA amended the charter to avoid stalemates with filibusters / The compromise agreed to allow the use of filibusters to delay votes on pervasive issues as long as the HOA member speaking continued to drink a beverage of the hosting chairperson's choice / This change to the charter caused half a dozen relapses but famously tabled a contentious mandatory poodle dying bill that would have otherwise easily passed if it wasn't for the decoration subcommittee chairwoman's love of sloe gin & soda / HOA meetings can get understandably out of hand following Fifth Fridays so the following weeks are usually kept sacred / The welcome subcommittee tries to hand out baskets of shortbread chessmen to new arrivals & those whose important causes fell / The Dandies feed Grief their cookies & fill out morning crosswords after a heated HOA meeting.

Run for the decoration subcommittee chair | turn to page 94

Help the chairwoman's election | turn to page 118

Blessed

by Mona Mehas

Blessed are the small creatures of the land
the wise rat, bringing gifts of wisdom and tenacity
the playful mouse, creative rabbit
spiders connecting vibrations with patience
snakes of spiritual intuition
protect them from those who misunderstand.

Blessed are the least of underwater creatures
krill that feed majestic whales
mosquito-devouring minnows
the adaptable octopus concealing its truth
salmon determined to spawn
protect them from human misuse.

Blessed are those occupying two worlds
transformative frogs, teaching us balance
persistent turtles following the currents
two-lined salamanders, skin for lungs
balanced in life, on land, and water
protect them from hidden dangers.

Blessed are navigators of the air
scissor-tailed flycatchers, nurturing warblers
bats of quiet esoteric magic
rebirthing of gentle luna moths
mastery and collaboration of bees in the hive
give them sweet life, protection from harm.

Untitled
by Susan L. Pollet

Collecting Cats
by Mona Mehas

When I was a child, I collected cats
not in the crazy cat lady fashion
but just enough to drive my mom
bonkers.

Nights when tomcats yowled after dark
I interrupted their loud arguments
and choosing the smallest cat I saw
picked him up.

Walking home from town with friends
a cat was stuck in a drainage pipe
rear-end visible, I pulled him out
took him home.

Behind the post office where I played
in the maintenance access was a cat
I don't recall how he got out
but he was mine.

Midnight, Joe, Red, Annabelle,
I'll never know what happened to them
they never came home, or we moved away
such was life.

There was one cat my mother liked
Tom-Tom chose to stay when we moved
she called and called his name that day
tears in my eyes.

In my sister's car, we drove away.

Maybe Honey

by Mona Mehas

Sad embrace of tears and sweat ruining my makeup
reaching my mouth

Worked so hard to apply with hands shaking and
heart racing but
we said goodbye

Sad embrace of soft fur in my hands when the
needle entered, I
just bought this new shade yesterday

His breathing labored, my
heart cried, my
ears bled

Sad embrace of his empty bed in my room, the
food donated, the
lonely walks

Trying to fathom the flavor of makeup and
tears and sweat
running into my mouth

Maybe honey

Tracking Our Animals

by Kate Falvey

I.

The raccoon
was early,
before the crowded trees
held only warblers
and the nattering of squirrels
pummeled the lake in glancing
dives, giving the grebes what for. Then
there were still tanagers, voicing
their globed remote golds when sly
winds smoothed back the beech leaves
and the squirrels were less feckless,
cobbing their cones of pine in silent
covertness, near stumps and hollows
that stored our water, fuel,
and light. We
were more primitive then
and always arrived glowing,
seeing less than we absorbed,
radiating all our thoughtless
wonder, innocent as rain.

These were the days of the orange
pup tent, the heavy skillet
and beaten coffee pot and
bacon smoking up in the morning
after a night stoking heat
in undulating covers. I
can still feel the young day
as a hand gently heeled to a
drowsy eye, the rouse of
orange wrapping spreading
its deepening wings,
the privacy almost unbearable,
the only thing better
than the limber, contemplative,

bosky air, an awful sheeting of
thunderous vexation
shivering us back into down.

The fires were always
stirring, magical --
rituals that I
could only lend a spirit to,
barred as I was from
axing and steepling the wood,
kindling the first dainty blaze
from courted shavings and chips,
choosing the least green timber
from the reverenced stack,
already split, and heaven-protected in the tarp,
raising the frame for the living flames
which always came unappeasable
into our world
drinking the night with fury,
claiming it by primordial right. You
were skilled in closing in a circle
for bright opulent splays of orange,
tooling upward scrolls of viridescent white
into lost-world caves and columns,
breathing as if by compact
an exalted shadow-making entity
into all of its elemental potency
onto a bidden site. You
never damped it down
but let it falter by itself,
guttering over the spent logs,
licking a last forked splinter
before billowing back to the dirt. You
might have had a flute
with a call silent to all but embers. You
watched, swigging starlight to the last,
long after I tucked loneliness
into bed, your real companion
a force unfelt by me. You
singed your eyebrows once
when rescuing a cramped
corner of a wasting flame
but that was later, after the

winds kicked mordantly up.

Here, in this soft dark,
we were just beginning
our orange nuptials and we
tilted toward each other
like birch surprised at their
adjacency. We
had not yet come
to grief and we
were fond and somewhat frolicsome. We
sat on a bench with a stalk of French bread
peering out of a sack. We
were possibly tired of cooking
on the sluggish hibachi, possibly
going to slice cheese or
spurt grapes into our bread-
dry mouths, possibly
planning to mix a salad
in the furrowed wooden bowl,
beefsteaks, cukes, and carrots
aired and piney, ready to rinse
and toss. We were
pausing, I know, and we were
certainly in New York, the
Catskills, perhaps, or the lower
Adirondacks. On a lake and not
a river so it was not
Uncle Pete's, the place of
tubing on the Esopus
where we learned about currents
and outcropping rocks. We may
have been enroute
from some place
to someplace else
and stopped here with our
hearty aplomb, our freedom,
and languid equipment. This
was before we had regular places,
destinations determined
by venturesomeness and love. This
was before we had more sporting
and experienced gear, a shelter

for the whole site so the rain
never muddied our entry or
enthusiasm. I have a notion
of a kind of compound
with strutting Winnebagos
strung with territorial lanterns and
hampered with makeshift porches,
like drawbridges to the
lawn chairs, welcome signs with
family names and caricatures,
card games and serious grilling
of neighborly spuds and steaks. We
pretended isolation,
secure in our baffled
dignity and growing infatuation
with the trees,
our lone tent tinily
out of place, but still
our dearest portion. We
were peaceably waiting
for one of us to move,
by mystic afferent impulse,
chore-ward, when
the 'coon
swooped our bread into the
piney hinterlands as swift
and neat as a kingfisher spearing
an unsuspecting perch.

The raccoons learned
to move on
when pickings
weren't as easy. They
deepened into the forest
where the boot soles weren't
as thick.

II.

The Moosehead bear
snuffled like a big raccoon
into our scrubbed and crumbless site.

The moonlight drifted spottily in
through the celadon canvas of our tent.
The huge lake misted the deep night pines
and the stillness was fast and unwondering.
The sound of a heart stopping snapped me
into the air. When my heart lumbered
into motion again it ran like quail
in tightening circles. I lay in my fear
thoughtlessly, zipped into my comfy
down home like a package of stiffening bait. Bears
don't particularly want to feast on flesh with any
fight left in it but the problem is, when one is
idle, helpless, and acutely conscious
of one's puniness,
that one, even schooled,
just really never knows. Now we
had had bear scares
before, like the one on the shores of
Cranberry where the dogs barked it off
and I listened in a half-sleep all night
for a graze of an unknown claw on stone. Or
the grizz in Jasper whose presence made us
switchback down the half-ascended trail,
knowing only that the steep
angles of the air were too seemingly unsprung,
the roots and trunks too seemingly freshly raked. And
on horseback once, in the Rockies again, the trees and plants
diminishing with our climb, a sighting following us up
the thin beauty of the peak like the smell of a truculent ghost.
We
pitched these scares between us like a tent, guywires
of shared tension and reason supporting our sheltering unity.

But Moosehead was different. No matter what
I knew of bears, I knew
you couldn't help us. The bear
sniffed for flecks of spice and blood.
You were so sound asleep
you never even heard.

III.

The moose had been rained on for days
covering himself with brush and nesting
in gusts of bent pine
branches. He was doused and in need of a run
to loose the leaves of maple and hemlock
from their tangle on his rack,
to spray the still-pent air with a drizzle
of haunch-matted pine needles. He wanted
warming and the electric friction of a
self-made wind in his glazy coat
but he hadn't bargained on the slim flick of road
being slick or even bleakly there or
the lone car goading itself
through the Rangeley mist with
a grudging curtailed onwardness,
its rain-punchy inhabitants
zinging drunken moose calls
into the leafy twilight
with a New York swagger and demand. We
had never in all our years in Maine
seen moose and today, caught in the car and
showered in thunderous grey,
we distracted ourselves by hurling our desires
to the silent pine sentries ranked
on either side of our way.

We saw the moose
jerk and hit the tar,
gravel bubbling up from our skid as we
stopped dead and speechless. He fell unbuffered,
with all his absolute might and regalness,
smack onto his broad bull-behind, his legs
spindling out crazily, his huge head swinging alarm
inches from our headlights. We
did nothing for a laden beat
then, in pell-mell simultaneity,
rolled our windows up and braced
for livid moose-assertion, the hoof or head
to the bumper, the crazing and shelling of
astonished windshield, our heads
cuffed and cracked like beech-nuts, relieved

of guilt and adrenalin. We
expected, deserved comeuppance
for having abetted the cause
of this pratfall. We wanted moose,
by golly, but never meant to spook one
into such ludicrous indignity. We
would have turned away
had we had time to sense
the outcomes. As it happened,
we bore witness and escaped
without a charge -- nary a withering moose-glare
nor bellowed scolding evening the score.
He collected his shocked but working limbs
and shook the road out of his head, then hightailed it
into the woods, hoping, we figured, that
none of his cows or cronies were around.

And down aways along our road
after a decent interval of silence, we
sputtered into laughs
convulsively
the way you shouldn't do
when something mighty
hits the dust. We
tweaked the story between us
when the thunder got too rough
and we savored
a knowing privilege,
sheepish but elite,
for stumbling on
this unaccustomed vision
of an addled nature
bumbling its
sublimity.

IV.

The elk condensed out of the vaporous
mountain dusk, moved into our range
and stood
still as a blessing poised
and unbestowed, staring into the

quickened light of our unrepentant
eyes. Our mugs of tea
steamed into the pause
and something
coalesced and cleared
and shone regenerate
and timeless
and there wasn't
any speaking
after she bowed and vanished
and after we set down
our
consecrated tea.

This happened where we
walked sidelong on glaciers
clamping our treads into the ice
and holding
for dear life.

Coda:

A vent on a cobbly grade in the lush Taconics
gives rise to huddles of leaf-loving families
trekking up-peak into mid-October, slowly,
movement its own end. I puff in the wake
of three capped and sweatered children,
their grandparents certainly our age,
preserved in the sweet-tempered,
renegade, macrobiotic look of,
god help us,
fifty years ago. I listen
as I climb, affecting more wind than I have,
to an enticing stream of encouraging babble. I
cup my listening and soon make out
observations and
invitations to observe,
explanations fanciful and actual,
a spill of buoyant skips and hops
and gentle, appreciative coaxing,
delight like the tumbles of orange leaves
spirited and spared by the softest of winds.

I prize a loop of fuzz from
a shard of granite and watch it
ride my palm. The oldest child,
a girl of perhaps eight, tells me
I'm holding a woolly bear. The woolly bear is black
with a middle of brown, or brown with edges of black.
The length of the winter is predicted
by the length of brown on the woolly bear.
The father, ponytail gangly and grey,
bandana slightly askew but expertly tied,
volunteers this bit
of lore, for which I am
ridiculously grateful.

We
had a kitten
together. You
rinsed her fear from her when I
cradled her into your arms
after the shaky car-ride, toweled
her off and let her
find her way
as she gingerly
rubbed herself home. You
took over
expertly, knowing
just how to be watchful
but unobtrusive, offering her safety
and independence, indulgence and fair,
essential limitation. She
curled against us when we slept
and I sang to her
as she rested on my belly. She
is still in her home
with you, grown sweet and lazy
with the name that I gave her.
She is still afraid of thunder
and she still flattens against you
at night, nosing into the warmth
of your always
being there.

I
haven't seen her
for years.
And, you know,
the woolly bear cautions
another long spell
of cold.

Zoo Story
by Kate Falvey

The great silverback
presses his haunches to the glass,
unfazed, chewing,
the amazed faces of children
a natural part of his terrain.

The children line the belled
viewing space
like a chattering fringe
of tropical primate.
They are easily reverent,
nudging, elbowing
only to alert
their fellows to
a fascinating monk
climbing the real
crenelated trunks
or combing real mites
from a crony's
coarse coat.

All adults are bayed
behind a railing,
officially warned to stay back
from the children.

Nick is
by far
the smallest,
except for the baby
gorilla latched
to ropes of hair or grasses.
He refuses
to turn
when we call,
fastened to the nearest clan of apes
as they make

off with their loping
uprightness
into the limited range of
our rescue.

Later,
down at the orang
habitat,
Jane, raised to be human
by a disaffected
rock star,
peers winsomely into the crowds,
courting affection with aggressive
refusal to rejoin
her own kind.

Mae
is wedged
on a stool before Jane's gaze,
her well-thumbed notebook full
of Jane's travail.
Freely feeding
facts and features of
orangutangia
to the questioning
curious,
it is clear
that she feels
she's on the wrong side
of the glass.

Still later,
Nick studies the ants
outside the lemur house
and, though there are no exhibit signs
with place of origin and Latin species
names and data,
ants
might well be
just
what we
came for.

Pigeons
by James B. Nicola

What changed my life one day was that I heard
what happened one hundred ten years ago
from one who owed her being to a bird.

Your first reaction hearing this: absurd,
right? How could that be, and how could she know?
I was suspicious too until I heard

about the village razed, survivors stirred
to action. World War One. You may well know
about the war, but not about the bird.

They used a homing pigeon to send word
to the next village, "Grab your kids and go!"
This saved the population since they heard

in time. Her tale continued. She assured
me that her grandfather, age ten or so,
lived in the village rescued by that bird.

Being both history buff and nature nerd,
I can't help but report, not that we owe
these pigeons in the park, but what I heard
of owing one's existence to one bird.

Beekeeping

Telling the Bees
by Colm O'Shea

The boy's family were gone, taken by the great Sickness. The brothers at the Abbey took him in. They were gentle souls, but they were old and serious men, their days set firm in routine: rising before dawn; prayer; rounds of chores; prayer; more chores; prayers; bed. They spoke often of God's love, and of great inner joy, which was God's gift, and maybe they really felt it. But there was no spark of play that children need to feel alive, loved, and at home. No one wrestled him like his older brothers, and he had no baby sister to tickle. Nobody sang him asleep as his mother had. If there's a god, the boy thought, he's little better than a thief in the night.

The closest thing to merriment in the Abbey was gathering for plainsong. The brothers stood shoulder-to-shoulder, chanting in a language the boy couldn't understand. Their low drone hummed off the chapel's stone walls.

"What's it mean?" the boy wondered. "Why does it sound so sad?" He suspected it just sounded sad to him. Maybe everything would seem sad from now on.

One day there was a buzz of excitement: Modomnoc was to visit the Abbey.

"Who?" asked the child. *Do you like sweet things, boy? Well so! Wait and see*, was their strange answer.

Modomnoc must have arrived as everyone slept, because the next morning when the boy roused from the dormitory, the old man was already there, greeting various brothers with hugs and laughter.

The boy stayed clear of the stranger, but watched him from afar. The old man was friendly, but spent much time alone, wandering the grounds, delight and wonder on his face as he inspected flower after flower.

A new sound entered the world after Modomnoc's arrival. Suddenly there were hundreds of bees. The tiny sisters hummed at their work from dawn to dusk, thronging the meadows that flanked the Abbey.

The days grew longer, brighter, more hopeful. The boy watched astonished as a large hive grew under the great oak by the Abbey graveyard. Everyone gave it a wide berth, but Modomnoc was a guest of honour with the sisters. They buzzed about him as he inspected the honeycombs, sampling their bounty with his finger, eyes closed in gratitude. The boy longed to approach this mysterious character, and ask him for that honey. But it felt overwhelming—asking too much.

"Do they never sting you?" the boy managed the courage to squawk from a safe distance one morning. Modomnoc came to, as if from a dream.

"Do my sisters sting me? They do not." He paused and then added: "I tell a lie. There was one time, early on when I was learning the art of beekeeping. But I took that as a blessing. And a warning."

"A warning?"

"Indeed. A dire warning—against pride, that first great sin. The sin the serpent in the tree put in me."

The boy soon learned one of the reasons Modomnoc was beloved: his honeybees helped the brothers make a drink called mead, which they stored reverently for special occasions. In their haste to harvest the honey before autumn, some monks tried to help the old man, but the bees stung the intruders horribly. Modomnoc was left alone with his humming convent. The boy saw him whispering to them often.

The boy yearned to learn the secrets of these whispers. One day he couldn't hold his tongue, and yelled from his safe perch in the hedge: "What are you telling the bees?!"

"I tell what's happening in our big human family. The local baptisms, marriages and deaths, and so on."

"Why?"

"The bees bridge worlds—between flowers and animals, between animals and man, and between man and the almighty. They're curious, and want to know the lay of the land. If they aren't told of the important events, they may take offense and leave."

The boy wanted to whisper to the bees, but he didn't have faith he'd be spared their terrible sting. He was no Modomnoc.

At night he dreamt of orders of bees, rising in circles around him, like great angelic orders. Were they upset he wasn't whispering to them? He wanted to tell them: my family is dead. My home is cold as stone.

Without warning or farewell, Modomnoc was gone. Suddenly it was autumn. A chill cut through the morning air as the boy inspected the hive. It had grown huge over the summer. He half-expected the bees to be gone too, vanished after their master, but no. They buzzed their plainchant inside and all around their own small chapel: a swarm of devotion.

Then, with no one around to witness, not even Modomnoc, the boy found himself weeping, and telling the bees everything he had lost, and would never get back. And after the bitter weeping, a great silence fell on him. The boy was so tired of this bitterness; he desperately wanted a taste of something sweet. Slowly, he approached the hive. He imagined the sisters swarming to kill the invader, because they had sworn to allow only the pure of heart take their honey. And he was no man of faith like Master Modomnoc. What was he at all?

As the boy reached out to the hive entrance, a pure dread entered his heart. The sun disappeared behind a cloud, and the world darkened.

He reached inside, ready for the stingers to pierce him, like tiny Roman soldiers with their swords, but he felt only tiny bodies part way for him. Then honey graced his touch. As he drew his hand back, the sun burst from the cloud, all the more dazzling. The amber light shone from his fingers, not of this world. The sweetest gift he'd ever tasted.

Peacock Lane's Queen Bee
by RJ Equality Ingram

She was a delight at her school dances but an absolute terror at the salad bar / She cleaned & reupholstered her designer handbags every weekend & spent her husband's money on shutting down fundraisers for causes she couldn't understand / Her hair was always out of fashion but framed her face in ways that made the style almost worth it / Every other weekend she'd pay a yuppie a crisp $100 to snip a couple times & say they touched it up / Food trucks she didn't like were driven out of business & the poor mime she used to harass at the farmers market was hit by a truck jay-walking away from her / Institutions crumbled beneath her pink kitten heels & locals learned to cross the street a block away from her semi-regular tantrums / She once tried speed dating on a singles cruise tailored to the divorced & two of her dates jumped overboard before the ship could dock / When she left her husband Mrs. Peacock Lane decided to get more involved in the community so she started the decoration subcommittee / It would become the child she would never have / She & her husband tried but it never worked & the renters who ran in & out of her house drove her mad / Lies about loving change dripped out of her mouth as she walked with The Dandies down the stairs to their unfinished basement where she found the roll top secretary with an old-fashioned lock that kept the panel shut / Go ahead / The Dandies offered her the key & when she saw their grief asleep inside a matchbox she wept / How unprepared we can become to watch another suffering so when the opportunity affords us we should always reach out instead of tearing down.

Ask Mrs. Peacock Lane to be grief's godmother | The End

Hacking

Peacock Lane Election Night
by RJ Equality Ingram

The Dandies almost ran a clean campaign against the chairwoman of the decoration subcommittee / They handed out red white & blue roses with little life hacks written around the stems like spells / Carry a pinch of salt in your back pocket for good luck & say aloud the names of your grandmothers / Rub aloe on your scalp after an upheaval for revival & bury a leek in the backyard the next time it rains / The neighborhood collected these roseate lessons & stuffed them in the bottom of their pockets like fortunes from fortune cookies or old lottery tickets scratched into oblivion / Steer clear of train tracks on Wednesdays & toss a penny into the next fountain you pass / Retire excuses with yesterday's wind & recite backwards the numbers you hated as a child / The Dandies filled the neighborhood with enough tiny spells to buttress a book of common prayer / It was a challenge for the chairwoman of the decoration subcommittee to rebuke such a charming campaign / The Dandies had shown everyone very briefly in kindness what years of torment from a sparkly gavel could not give / Their words stitched back together a kind of fondness for the unseen Peacock Lane held onto only in dreams / The Dandies won their HOA election by a landslide because of their roses & the stand they took against the subcommittee's stale right hand & became the new co-chairs of the decoration subcommittee / The Stranger walked Mrs. Peacock Lane home after it was all over to make her some tea & offered to help her play nice with the neighbors / If you treat every decoration like it's a Christmas decoration & every neighborhood like a tourist destination then everything will come with its own joy.

Leave out a tin of fish & hope the cats come back | The End

Mariposa Effect
by Lores Denison

FADE IN:
INT. OFFICE - DAY

An empty, open-plan office decorated in modern millennial gray, the logo for Hi-Hai painted on the wall behind the reception desk.

TILDA (30s) sits at this desk typing random letters while trying to eavesdrop on JORDYNNE (20s) who is talking animatedly on the phone in the glass corner office.

> TILDA
>
> OMG! Look at me! I'm Jordynne with a 'y' and two 'n's.
> I'm so clever and perfect! Sun shines out my ass!

Jordynne catches Tilda's eye, smiles, and gives a thumbs up through the glass wall. Tilda returns the gesture with a fake smile.

Jordynne hangs up and comes out of the office with her matching coat and handbag.

> JORDYNNE
>
> OMG. Michael loved our work!

> TILDA
> (under her breath)
>
> My work.

> JORDYNNE
>
> I'm going to get an acai bowl from next door. You want to come?

> TILDA
>
> No thanks, I'm all set.

She holds up a brown paper lunch sack.

> JORDYNNE
>
> Perf! You can stay and man the phones. What would I do

without you, Tilly?

Jordynne leaves out the door. We hear her heels clicking down the hall and then the elevator ding.

Tilda unwraps her pb&j and is just biting into it when the phone rings. She looks at it, then her sandwich, then reluctantly sets down her sandwich and picks up the phone.

> TILDA
>
> Hi-Hai Language Solutions, this is Tilda. How may I help you?

A smooth AI VOICE answers

> VOICE
>
> Matilda Raymundo.

> TILDA
>
> Yes? And this is...?

> VOICE
>
> We know what you're doing, you clever girl.

> TILDA
>
> Sorry?

> VOICE
>
> Don't worry, Matilda, we won't tell anyone about your little code patch. But in exchange we would like you to do something for us.

> TILDA
>
> Who is this?!

> VOICE
>
> Your supervisor just left for lunch. It's work from home Friday, and you're alone in the office. Do this for us now, and we won't tell your boss what you've been up to with the foreign currency exchanges.

> TILDA
>
> Are you watching me?

VOICE

In the outer pocket of your backpack is a flash drive.

Tilda reaches down into her backpack and pulls out a nondescript royal blue flash drive, stunned.

TILDA

How did you-

VOICE

Go into Ms. Hollis' office and log in to her computer. We know you know the password, you sneaky girl. Put the drive into her computer and click 'run' in the pop-up window. It should take 20 minutes. When it's finished, log out and put the flash drive in your lunch bag. When you leave work at 5:30, go for your walk around the park as usual. When you pass the trashcans by the charging station, drop the paper bag in the paper recycling bin. Finish your lap and then get into your car and leave immediately. Do you understand?

TILDA

This is creepy. I'm calling the police.

VOICE

Are you sure you want to get the police involved, Matilda? If you do this for us, we won't tell your boss or the police about your secret skimming project. Do you understand?

TILDA

What's on the flash drive?

VOICE

You don't need to worry about that, Matilda, but the clock is ticking. Do we have a deal?

TILDA

What proof do you have?

VOICE

Matilda, this little favor we're asking won't cost you anything at all. But if you don't do as we say, you could lose everything. Is it really worth it to question us

                              TILDA

          Fine. I'll do it.

                              VOICE

          Thank you.

There is a click as the call ends.

Tilda looks at the clock and then walks into the glass office with the drive.
She logs in, plugs in the drive, hesitates for a second, but then starts running
the program. A green percentage bar shows up on the screen.

As the numbers steadily climb, Tilda goes back to retrieve her sandwich and
eats it while watching the screen.

Finally the bar shows 100% and Tilda grabs the drive and logs out hastily.
We hear the elevator ding in the hall.

She is about to leave when she notices jelly residue on the CTRL key. We can
here Jordynne's heels clicking again, getting closer.

                              TILDA

          Shit. Shit.

She licks her thumb and wipes the jelly off, then hurries out of the office
back to her desk.

Jordynne walks in with a to-go bag.

                              TILDA
                            (Too loud)
          Hi! Hi-Hai acai...bowl.

                            JORDYNNE
                       (startled and confused)
          Hi? Any calls?

                              TILDA
          Nope! Nopey dopey. How about you? Any calls? I mean.
          Nope!

She laughs awkwardly.

JORDYNNE
I'm going back to my office now.

Jordynne steps away and Tilda sighs. She looks at the flash drive and notices for the first time a butterfly symbol etched into it. She shoves it into her paper bag.

EXT. - PARK - DAY

Tilda is walking through a city park. She keeps a quick pace and keeps peeking over her shoulders. She looks at everyone she passes with suspicion - a young woman pushing a toddler in a stroller, an old man with a cane, a jogger, a dog-walker.

She reaches a recycling bin and shoves the paper bag in there, then takes off walking again.

She arrives at her car, unlocks it, gets in, and slams the lock shut.

She exhales and looks at her phone - a message from Mika reads: See you tonight, sexy! ;*

She smiles and starts the car.

INT. - LIVING ROOM - NIGHT

MIKA (30s) and Tilda are sitting on the floor at the coffee table, eating from takeout containers.

MIKA
And you have no idea who it was or how they knew so
much about you?

TILDA
(shaking her head)
Or how they even got into my backpack.

The hint of relief passes across Mika's face, before she wipes it with one of concern.

TILDA
That's what freaks me out the most. That they could get so
close to me. I feel violated. The same as when my neighbor
started stalking me back in Houston.

Mika looks alarmed and pained and maybe a bit guilty at this.

                              MIKA
          Did anyone bump into you at the park? Or maybe they
          snuck it in while you were in the bathroom in a cafe?

                              TILDA
          Maybe.

                              MIKA
          I'm going to make you a drink.

Mika places her hand on Tilda's shoulder and slides it down her arm to her
hand.

                              MIKA
          And then I'm going to make you forget all about flash
          drives.

They smile at each other and share a kiss. Their kiss grows more passionate
and the reach for each other.

                              TILDA
          Let's forget about the drinks.

Tilda stands, and holds her hand out for Mika. Mika takes it and stands as
well. They kiss as they walk toward the bedroom.

In her enthusiasm, Tilda bumps into an end table, knocking Mika's purse to
the floor. Pens, lip balm, tampons, and other items scatter across the carpet.

                              TILDA
          Oh, shit, I'm sorry.

Tilda turns to begin to pick up the mess.

                              MIKA
          Leave it.

She begins to draw Tilda in for another kiss, but something catches Tilda's
eye - a royal blue flash drive. She picks it up and flips it over to see a butterfly
symbol etched there.

                         TILDA

Mika?

Mika looks terrified.

                         MIKA

Baby, it's not what it looks like.

                         TILDA

What the fuck does it look like? Why was this in your
purse?

Tilda begins to back away. Mika holds her hands out in a conciliatory man-
ner.

                         TILDA

Who are you? Have you been - what? - spying on me?

She gasps.

                         TILDA

Have you been *playing* me?

                         MIKA

No, baby! I care about you I would never hurt you!

                         TILDA

But you would blackmail me?

                         MIKA

It's not like that. Let me explain.

                         TILDA

You'd better explain. What is on this flash drive? And why
did you threaten me about our secret project? It was your
idea!

                         MIKA

It wasn't me on the phone. It was my boss.

                         TILDA

Darren? From the driving instruction agency? Why would
he want to ruin my life?

MIKA

They would never tell anyone! They were just bluffing!

TILDA

They? Who the fuck is they?

Mika exhales deeply and looks Tilda in the eyes.

MIKA

I work for an organization.

Tilda finally stops backing up and stares at Mika.

TILDA

An organization?

Mika runs both hands through her hair.

MIKA

You weren't supposed to find out, but I'll tell you. We're called Mariposa. It's a kind of collective. People with different... skills come together and try to bring about change by exposing the rich and powerful. I help them out sometimes.

TILDA

By teaching teenagers how to drive?

MIKA

That's just cover. But yeah, it's a good one. Makes surveillance easy. Different cars every day. And then when they found out I was dating you, they asked if I could help with this mission.

TILDA

Mission?

MIKA

Jordynne, your boss? She's dating a really sleazy guy. A politician. Chaz Hamish. He mismanaged the funds for wildfire relief efforts a few years back. My superiors suspect he took advantage of the tragedy to line his own pockets, but they need proof. And so far, your connection to Jordynne was the closest we've been able to get. The flash drive has mirroring malware on it. We were hoping to find something incriminating within social media or email correspondence.

> TILDA

This is a lot.

> MIKA

I'm so sorry, baby! I never meant to scare you. I didn't think how it might be triggering for you. I was just trying to make the world a better place.

She looks down, dejected.

> TILDA

Why didn't you just ask me to help?

Mika looks up.

> MIKA

What?

> TILDA

If this guy is as horrible as you say, why didn't you just ask me to help you?

Mika stutters.

> TILDA

Plus, I'm not sure you'll get much off of Jordynne's work computer. You'd do better to infect her phone. It would take some finesse, but I sure I could get access to her phone somehow.

> MIKA

You want to help?

> TILDA

Why not? You're not the only one who wants to save the world. Besides, you know how much I hate Jordynne.

They smile at each other.

                    MIKA
          Okay. I'll introduce you to my boss.

BEGIN MONTAGE

-- It's night in an empty parking lot. Tilda and Mika step out of a car and walk towards MIKA'S BOSS, a shadowy figure in a trench coat. Tilda and Vanessa shake hands.

-- Tilda and Mika and Mika's boss sit in a dark corner of a dive bar, discussing plans, writing in a notebook.

-- Tilda sits at her desk in the office, typing code. When Jordynne walks by she smiles at her and compliments her outfit.

INT. - LIVING ROOM - NIGHT

Tilda sits on the couch typing on her laptop. Mika brings her a glass of wine and joins her on the couch.

Tilda gives a final keystroke with a flourish.

                    TILDA
          I think that's it.

                    MIKA
          You finished?

                    TILDA
          Yeah. It's ready to go.

                    MIKA
          Tomorrow, then?

                    TILDA
          Yeah, tomorrow.

                    MIKA
          Cheers to that.

They clink their wine glasses together.

INT. - OFFICE - DAY

Tilda is at her desk. She's watching Jordynne through the glass of her office.

She pulls up a QR code onto her phone and takes a deep breath.

She walks to Jordynne's office.

> TILDA

Hey girl!

> JORDYNNE

Hey!

> TILDA

I was just wondering if you could help me out and do a
quick test of our new QR codes for me? Do you have your
phone? I just want to make sure they work before I update
our site.

Tilda holds up the QR code on her phone.

> JORDYNNE

Sure thing! Just a sec.

She gets out her phone and scans the code. She receives an error message on
her phone. She turns it around to show Tilda.

> JORDYNNE

Uh oh! Someone's got more work to do!

> TILDA

Oh darn. I guess I messed up something. Let me go fix
that!

She backs out of the office. When she turns around, she smiles. She pops a
quick text to Mika: We're in.

INT. - BEDROOM - DAY

Tilda is in bed asleep. Her phone buzzes and dings. She squirms and grabs
her phone. She reads it sleepily.

Mika walks in with two coffee mugs. She hands one to Tilda and gets back in
bed.

> MIKA

Good morning, sexy.

                    TILDA

Good morning indeed.

Tilda grabs the remote and turns on the T.V.

On the screen, we can see footage of Chaz Hamish being led out of a build-
ing by police.

                  NEWS ANCHOR
Early this morning, State Senator Chaz Hamish was ar-
rested on 32 charges of corruption including conspiracy,
bribery, wire fraud, money laundering, and filing false tax
returns.

Tilda and Mika cheer.

                    TILDA

We did it!

                    MIKA

You did it.

They kiss.

The screen changes to show Jordynne being escorted by police.

                    TILDA

Is that?

                  NEWS ANCHOR
Hamish and his companion may be facing additional
felony charges for possession of narcotics, which were
found in his home during the course of the arrest.

Tilda's phone dings again. She checks it.

                  NEWS ANCHOR
The charges and arrests may have upset Hamish's plans to
run for Senate in the next election, as Republican party
leaders are beginning to withdraw their support.

                    TILDA

I think I just got promoted.

MIKA

It's about damn time.

They clink mugs and take sips.

MIKA

What are you going to do about our secret project?

TILDA

I already nixed it.

MIKA

And the money?

TILDA

Donated to disaster relief.

Mika kisses her cheek. Tilda turns to her.

TILDA

So. Who next?

FADE OUT.

THE END

Classics

Marble Inscription, Roman, archeological musuem, Turkey

by Roger Camp

Alice in Winter

by Kate Falvey

Shove over, Dinah, and get your whiskers
out of my tea. There's not enough cream
at this picnic for the two of us and I have dibs

on the scones. Or maybe the scones are ethereal
and multiply, loaf-and-fish-like, and will serve
me, you, and visions, too, if that rabbit flickers by,

fob a-glinting. And, now I squint more closely,
you are looking rather drab and squirrel-fuzzy
and a might translucent, too, hazy as belief,

the heather peering through your drift of calico.
It really can't be you unless you are a shadow of
your former self. Or maybe you're an elf, those ears

too kittenish for decorous old cat-dom to be sure. Sly-
boots, you are, drifting in on fog, dodo feathers trickling
from your maw. You're not at all how I recall, more

skeletal and skulking-- in a drowsy starveling way – the bones
more elongate and filmy, the skull no longer pertly, vaguely
heart-shaped, just vague and rather chilling. In fact, I find

myself uneasy and you're not helping me one whit as you
purr into the void of this flurried afternoon. And I might
swoon into girlhood in this oddly feral heat and snip some

of the fight out of those caterwauling daisies but it's so
bothersome to try to braid such swaying clumsy stems
into a chain that tethers only to its own flimsy invisibility.

Choose Your Own Unhappy Endings

by Lavinia Darr

after Margaret Atwood's "Happy Endings"

You've heard this tale a thousand times in a thousand different ways, but there was a girl thousands of years ago on some stupid island or peninsula whose face launched a thousand ships.

.

The story starts, as always, with Zeus. Either it starts because he turns himself into a swan and knocks up Queen Leda with Castor, Pollux, and Helen, or it starts when he wants to stir some shit and picks some random second-born Trojan prince to decide which of three goddesses are the most beautiful. The goddesses try to bribe the prince in a bunch of different ways, but Aphrodite promises him the most beautiful woman in the world.

He takes her up on her offer.

Somehow that's still Helen's fault.

.

Helen was the princess of Sparta and had already been abducted once already to be the child bride of some other demigod, but her brothers rescued her. Her father still sold her off to the highest bidder. That's the long and short of every minute of her life.

Helen was married to Menelaus and:

Helen is happy with Menelaus. Aphrodite gives her to Paris anyway.

or

Paris abducts Helen while she was screaming and crying and rapes her.

or

Paris was a suitor she preferred while she was being paraded around, but Menelaus won her hand which is ridiculous because he wasn't even there.

or

Helen never wanted to marry at all, but that didn't matter to anyone.

Not once was she asked.

The outcome is the same: Helen of Sparta is married to Paris of Troy, and her face launches a thousand ships.

.

Agamemnon was there in Menelaus's stead when her father was courting suitors for her. Agamemnon ended up marrying her sister and sacrificing her niece for better weather, and that's her fault too. Blood for weather. Blood for war.

Her sister hates her ship-launching face and hates her husband-brother-in-law's murderous hands, so she slits his neck for killing their daughter, and then their son slits hers for killing his father. Blood begets blood begets blood.

.

The war goes on and on and on. One thousand ships and ten thousand deaths.

.

Troy's descendants will say that there was a gift given under false pretenses filled with soldiers, and:

Helen betrays Troy and distracts Trojan soldiers with her beauty so the Greeks can bring her home, or the other way around, but having a face people are distracted by isn't a choice.

or

Helen sits inside with the white-armed Andromache and laments in silence. Spartan women are steel-armed not white-armed. She was supposed to be a warrior or a hunter, not trapped inside like a little wife.

or

Helen sits out the war in Egypt. The gods send a doll in her place to Troy. If that was an option the whole time, they should have just given Paris a doll in the first place. That's all he really wanted. Both sides really.

.

Hector kills Patroclus so Achilles kills Hector so Paris shoots Achilles' heel so an archer shoots Paris. Troy burns. Helen does nothing, which if you've noticed she has done beautifully throughout. It is all she is allowed to do.

.

The Greeks enslave Andromache, and Odysseus throws her baby from the battlements—or maybe the baby grows up and kills him, or maybe he adopts the baby and raises him as his own, or maybe the baby grows up to fuck his mother and kill his father. Oh wait, wrong story.

.

After Troy burns:

Helen is sent home to Menelaus, and he kills her.

or

Helen is sent home to Menelaus, and they never speak of

Troy again.

or

Helen is raped and killed in Troy by either the Greeks or the Trojans in a rage.

or

Aeneas finds her in the burning of Troy, but Aphrodite saves her life. She never once asked to be saved.

or

Her niece Iphigenia sacrifices her to a god. How's that for fair play?

or

Helen is taken by Apollo to Mount Olympus because she's a demigod too. And fuck the Greeks and Trojans anyway. And fuck Menelaus too.

or

Helen has no idea what's going on in Troy or Sparta because she's in Egypt.

When Troy burns, Helen is too far away to smell the smoke or hear the wailing in the streets or the moaning of the men trapped under their own buildings and battlements. She hunts deer with her daughter, who got to come with her this time and was never forgotten about or abandoned. Iphigenia was never sent to her father's sacrificial altar on her wedding day under false pretenses, and instead makes flower crowns from the Nile-side lotuses. Clytemnestra is there, sipping wine with Cassandra—who, while we're dreaming, was never enslaved and never survived a god spitting lies in her mouth. Hell, Dido is there too, and she never burns. Medusa is never beheaded. Medea never kills her children. Philomela's tongue is never cut out, and she and her sister are never turned into birds. Eve hears all this good news and wings it over from Eden. When she shares fruit with Pandora, neither of them are blamed for man's follies.

When Cassandra speaks of happy endings here, the women in this ending get to believe what she says. They get to believe they're not just an instrument in some man's epic poem, but the masters of their own fate.

Dorothy, Alice, and Red in the Wild

by Kate Falvey

I. Forest Blues

The grab of trees is nothing.
I'm hip to their enchantments,
their impenetrable leavings; they ought
to be less obvious when calling the winds
for a ride. Their branches out them every time.
There is always one struggling to smother a laugh,
always a pair curving like arms, always a skeletal
beckoning, a threat of tearing and ultimate capture.

I roll my eyes and barely glance their way.
You'd think by now they'd know
I'll never lose my stride.
(You'd think they'd shift allegiances and
choose the better side.)

II. Scones with Dinah on the Riverbank

Ok, Girls, here's the scoop.
Snouts and muzzles aren't tricks of the light.
There are fangs aplenty
glinting through the cattails
as you spread your checkered cloth
upon the dewy sedge
and invite your cat to tea.

III. Through the Woods

Swing the basket in extravagant loop de loops,
piecrusts cracking and jam jars bruising the fruit.
The old girl never expected compliance.
She whooped it up and snapped
her lacy garters in her youth.

She takes in the burrs and seedpods
on the lusty scapegrace cape and
hungers for the wolf.

Peacock Lane | Classic
by RJ Equality Ingram

Gosh what a couple of egg heads those Goths were / A real match forged in cartoonish annihilation / They were the talk of the neighborhood for the better part of the season & shook all the pine needles down to weave baskets for their Chinese-crested named Thing / Then as quickly as they came round they were outta here / We were watching claymations on our desktops when the ice in our glasses started clinking / The Mrs. She overanalyzes half the patterns when their long black hearse pulled up & they started loading their coffin shaped furniture / That that gothic couple was the best of us / Real sweet hearts / They fit right in beautifully kinda contrasting what the rest of us are doing with our outlandish but more traditional decorating / But that poor Shelly went a bit tilted trying to ruin their lives didn't she? / I heard it ended in a couple of restraining orders & drove poor Morticia & Gomez straight outta town she did / But the Mrs. Addams chic—who was really lovely by the way—did this big showy spell in front of the house & it scared the Jesus out of Shelly / Mrs. Addams recited beatnik poetry & scuttled around completely in character & she stopped & pulled her dress up & revealed her nylons right in front of the whole jolly gosh darn Christmas light jamboree & then vanish outta here in her hearse leaving that sexy leg lamp as a housewarming present for the next masochists who try to tête-à-tête with Mrs. Peacock Lane / And these new gentlethems in top hats & monocles have really been playing par for the course against this very unique menace to society who is in her own way a beautifully underachieving supervillain with limitless creativity in a hot pink pant suit & a stash embroidered PEACOCK LANE. | The End.

Lucy, do you remember when we bathed together?

by Abigail Ray

You were maroon and indigo
A kaleidoscope of a person
Your body floated like clouds
And you looked at me like something with wings and feathers
You looked like starlight encircling planets
Like you left moonbeams instead of footprints
I loved you like a cloud, like something just passing through.
But if clouds are just vapor
(Just water and sugar - so much like tears)
Can I be aloft in you? Can I float up from a lonely cup of water
on some poor saps nightstand?
Or rain from a puddle?
Or dew off morning dandelions?
Whatever shape I take I still spell out your name.

The Marble Halls of Arts & Letters Book 2

by timothy arliss obrien

Chapter 1: Concrete Poems on the theft of Euterpe's Elixir

1. INTRODUCTION: THE FALL OF BALANCE
Before the Halls of Marble cracked,
      before the muses wept ink into the veins of the Academy,
         there was harmony.

The gods whispered inspiration through gilded corridors,
      and the students drank deeply of creation's endless well.
But one among them—Professor Moros—grew restless.
    He saw not a gift but a **shackle**,
       not a blessing but a **barrier**.

Why should creativity bow to unseen hands?
    Why must art remain a vessel for divinity when it could
be more?
In the deep hours, beneath the stone vaults of the Library
    accessible only through a hidden stairwell in the
Letterpress Lab
      he ventured.
        (seeking the secret)

He traced the forgotten sigil. He broke the seal.
And thus, the world began to unravel.

2. ASCENSION: (THE HORRORS OF THE THIEF BEGIN)

  Δ
there is an idea born into man
which becomes myth
Ω
    which becomes legend
  ∞
    — He descends —
the staircase {unbuilt}

                the air thickening
                        the case against him builds
            (the door ahead)
             (the void beyond)
       « the elixir sings »
              ♫
    ☉   *ψ*
        it sings
             it
                (wails)
                    it wails
                —> TOO LOUD TOO LOUD TOO LOUD

« THE INK EVERYWHERE BLEEDS BACKWARD »

        π
« the gods cannot follow »
                cannot
                    (will not)
                        dare not

. . .
(the numbers fracture)
(the song unwinds)
(the end begins)

3. THE KEY TURNED IN THE LOCK

      (11)
        Ω
    —   9   —

        ‖‖‖
        ‖‖‖   The door stood still
        ‖‖‖   until he whispered the name
    — + + —
          φ
        (7)
△ △ △ △ △ △
      Ω
      Ω   (No mortal should know it)
      Ω   [a deep forgotten sigil]
      Ω   *The word older than breath*
      Ω
      Ω   ⊘   *The sign that unbinds*
      Ω

Ω ⊖   *The name that unlocks*
Ω
Ω ⊗   *The word that should have stayed buried*
Ω
(5)
Δ Δ Δ Δ Δ Δ
  — 3 —
    ‖‖
    ‖‖   The door did not creak.
    ‖‖   It did not hesitate.
  — 1 —
    Ω

4. THE CHALICE UPON THE ALTAR

          (Δ)
        (✦ ❀)
        (. ° ✧)
        (✧ *.° ☆)
        (⊗   ⊗   )
        (☆   *. ☽   )
                  |
         | |
         | GOLD |
         | TOO MUCH |
         | TOO BRIGHT |
         | |
         | |
         | a word |
         \ a song /
          \ a color /
           \   /
            \ a   /
            \curse/
             \   /
              \ /
               *
             *   *
             *   *
            *   *
           *   *
          *   *
         *   *
        *   *
       *   *
      *   *
*CREATIVITY ***
*****SLIPS** *

```
*      *AWAY*
 * **FROM**
   *  **** *
    *  THE  *
    *  GODS  *
    *          *

   *            *

  ** FOREVER* *
  **************
```

5. **communion of the elixir**

(He drinks the cup empty)
            he drowns in the well

gold turns s=i=l=e=n=t +

        echoes spiral
                (outward inward both neither)
    Δ – Ω =   ☆ ☽
       the *muses*   (unwoven)

all power slips through his fingers
            ||||| ||||| |||||
            (a vessel unmade)
            (a mouth unmoored)
            (a name unwritten)
              ☆ ★ ☆ ★ ☆

6. 6. 6. THE THREAD UNMAKING (⊘, ⊖, ⊗, ⊞)

Δ   *Σ*

            (crack)
Ω   *φ*
   the loom breaks
  ⊘   ⊖   ⊗
        — 3 —
   threads (u n r a v e l)
              6
```
```

words   (c o r r o d e)
        - φ -
  9   *shadows ^{spill} out*
     Σ

Ω (a single thread remains) | | (they pull) | (they pull) | | | (the loom does not protest) | |
Ω (but the price is) | | **everything** | | **a name erased** | |
a god unmade | |
Ω (the tapestry flutters once) (and then—) | |

⊗ ⊖ ⊘
   time
folds
     (again)
─────────── (again)
               (again)
          (thunder breaks in the distant) ───────
Ω Ω Ω Ω Ω Ω Ω Ω Ω
     He is the artist now
     He is the ruin now
   [He is the fates now]

7. THE SKY SHATTERS

Ω Ω Ω Ω Ω Ω Ω Ω Ω
✈ ❀ .°˚ ✧ ✧.₀ ☆ ☆ *. ☽ *
   * * * * * * * * * * * *

- -
     (THE VEIL)
       (TEARS)
         (THE FABRIC)
          (SPLITS)
            (THE TIDES)
             (REVERSE)
              (THE GODS)
   *. ☽ * ✧   (LOOK AWAY)
   *
   *✈ ❀ .°˚ ✧ ☆ ★ *. ☽ * ★ ★ ☆ ✧ *.₀ ☆ ☆ *. ☽ *
   Ω Ω Ω Ω Ω Ω Ω Ω Ω

     THE PAINTINGS BURN
        THE POETS FORGET [WORDS]

THE MUSIC TURNS ~~STATIC~~
THE STARS LOSE THEIR _{NAMES}

A HAND REACHES THROUGH
AND TAKES WHAT WAS

NEVER MEANT

~~TO BE HELD~~

Ω Ω Ω Ω Ω Ω Ω Ω Ω

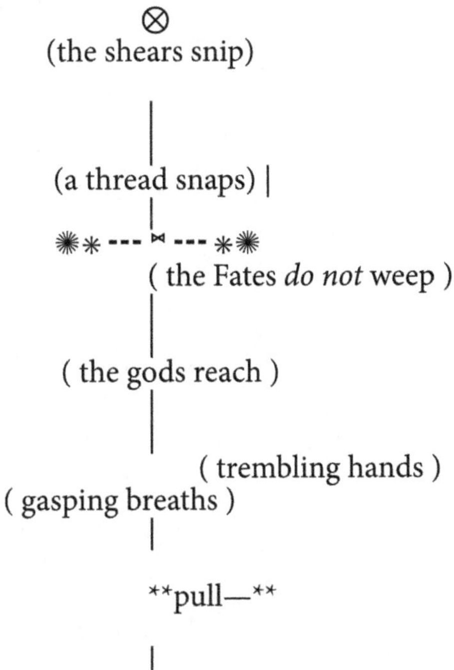

Ω Ω Ω Ω Ω Ω Ω Ω Ω
8. the gods do what they can

⊗

(the shears snip)

|

(a thread snaps) |

✳✳ --- ⋈ --- ✳✳
(the Fates *do not* weep)

(the gods reach)

(trembling hands)
(gasping breaths)

pull—

|

125

twist—

|

tie—

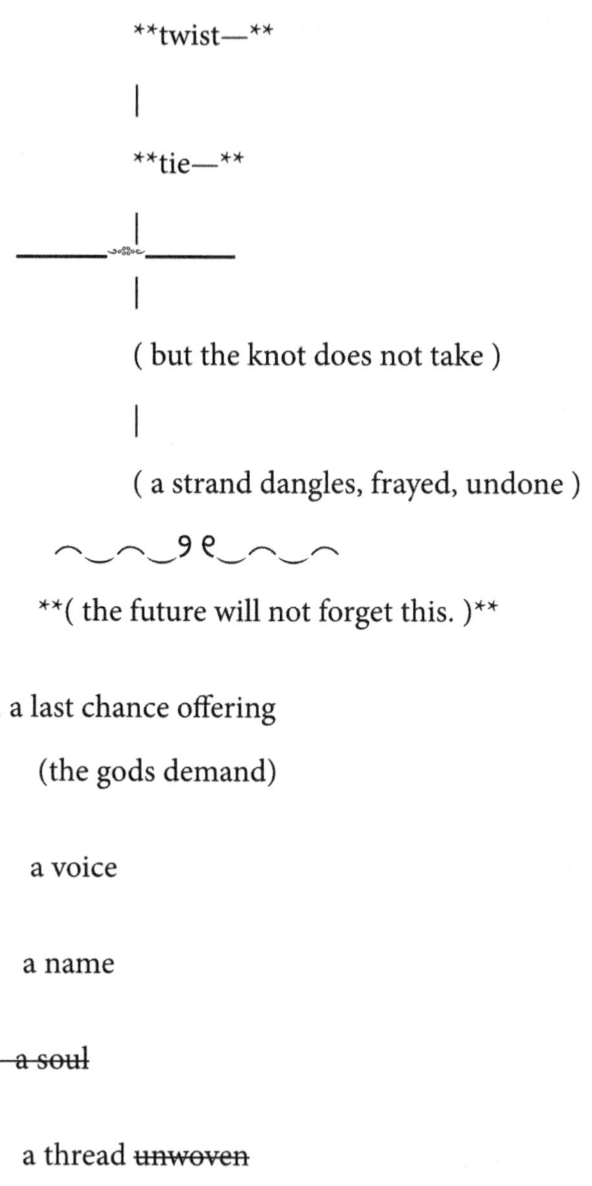

(but the knot does not take)

|

(a strand dangles, frayed, undone)

(the future will not forget this.)

9. a last chance offering

   (the gods demand)

  a voice

  a name

—a soul

  a thread unwoven

  (the students arise)

  "take us instead."

silence.

the gods consider.

the abyss opens.

(something falls)

(something is taken)

(something is forever gone)

the loom hums again

fate breathes once more.
~~we will never know what was lost~~

10. EXORDIUM: THE TRIAL OF MOROS

When the fabric of fate was frayed, when inspiration ran dry as dust, when the fates turned their faces from the halls of creation—every part of the universe itself was compelled to act.

The Academy trembled. The stars, who had long stood as silent witnesses, murmured among themselves. The moon, pale and ever-watchful, waxed full with judgment. The rivers ceased their song. The wind carried no word across the firmament.

A crime had been committed.

A thief had risen beyond his appointed station.

Professor Moros, breaker of threads, desecrator of the muses, stood accused.

And so, the celestial court was called.

The scales of justice, hidden behind mortal sight, tilted into equilibrium. The constellations aligned, forming an unbroken sigil. From the depths of Tartarus to the peaks of Olympus, from the ink-stained archives of the Academy to the endless halls of marble, all were summoned.

- The **Fates**, weavers of destiny, arrived with their tapestry tattered,
- its edges burned where his hand had grasped at what was forbidden.
- The **Muses**, hollow-eyed and grieving,
- whispered accusations in tongues once brimming with poetry.
- The **Gods**, luminous and unyielding, bore witness with eyes that saw too much.
- The **Students**, the ones who had lost and fought and sacrificed, stood at the threshold, trembling but unbroken.

At the center of it all, bound in chains spun from **dark disastrous stories and undone fates**, stood Moros. The fallen professor who sought to **rewrite the order of inspiration**, to steal the divine gift.

The question now remained—

Would the universe permit his existence?

Would the stars allow his name to be spoken again?

Would the act of creation, once defiled, be restored?

The trial began.

Chapter 2:

Courtroom Transcript - The Case of Stolen Elixir

Opening Statements:
The Honorable Justice Themis presiding over the Court of Creativity:

Ladies and gentlemen of the Academy,
In this hallowed court of creativity,
We gather to unveil a tale most daunting,
A saga wrought within the shadows haunting
of our sacred institution of artistic longing.

Professor Moros, a seeker in our midst,
In pursuit of an elixir's whispered lore,
Broke an oath and tore open a sacred door,
losing our trust, forevermore.

The elixir, a potion with a mystic hue,
Hid in the sacred halls where inspiration grew,
Promising true artistry, yet leaving shadows in its wake,
Became his cursed quest leaving our very balance at stake.

Through witnesses and words, truths we shall glean,
In the court of creativity
once we reach justice
we may convene.

Opening statements by
The Prosecution team of Mount Olympus:

Your honor,
        We stand here today to bring forth evidence,
Against professor Moros, who, driven by an insatiable quest for
power, plotted to locate the forbidden Elixir of Euterpe within
the sacred halls of the Academy, exercised esoteric dark arts to
open the seal locking the chamber away for our protection, and
then partook of the forbidden substance.

Opening Statements by
The Defense team for Professor Moros:

Your honor,
bear witness not just to the crime, but to the wound;
a wound that bleeds ink and oil, verse and vision,
the silent suffering of those who burn too brightly.

You call this professor a thief, yet was he not a surgeon,
reaching into the frayed loom of fate where the muses at times
turn cruel,

where the gift of creation twisted into a slow unraveling in the minds of humans?
Too many have fallen— Van Gogh by his own trembling hand, Plath by the hush of the gaslight, Rothko bleeding into the floor, Woolf wading into the river's cold embrace, Arbus lost behind the camera's final flash, Hemingway with a shotgun's last punctuation, Cobain with the echo of his own refrain, Gorky hanging between ruin and memory, Francesca Woodman vanishing mid-frame—brilliance turned to dust, the gift of creation twisted into an unbearable weight.

Professor Moros did not steal out of greed, but out of desperation, to patch the gaping hole where genius becomes grief, where inspiration devours instead of ignites.
He saw the abyss yawning at the feet of his students, and in defiance of the gods, he reached for the only cure. Do not call this heresy—call it an act of love."

The Honorable Justice Themis:
Thank you both.
Please bring forward the Witnesses.

Witness One: **The Painter – Sofia**
"I painted in the sanctum of color until my fingers blistered, until the smell of turpentine clung to my skin like a second soul. My own reflection vanished behind the canvases—I was only the hands that worked, the eyes that saw, the mind that unraveled. I tried to tell my professors, the muses, the gods, but they only called it unbridled passion. But Moros—he took the brush from my shaking fingers and made me step back. He made me see how much of myself I had already lost. He stayed with me in the empty studio, washed the paint from my hands when I was too weak to do it myself, he sighed, 'If only we had the elixir, you could create without becoming a sacrifice.'"

Witness Two: **The Musician – Linus**
"The music wouldn't stop. It rattled the walls of the grand hall and inside my ribs and scraped against my skull and played behind my eyes even when my hands were too raw to bring forth another note. My body broke trying to keep up, my mind cracked under the weight of every unfinished melody. Moros found me in the studio of noise one night, shaking, my fingers bleeding into the ivory and strings, and he took my hands in his

own. He whispered that music was meant to heal, not harm, that the gods were cruel to let it consume me. And then, with sorrow in his voice, he said, 'If only we had the elixir, I could quiet the storm inside of you.'"

Witness Three: **The Poet – Phoebe**
"The words never let me rest. They came in torrents, in whispers, in screams, until I couldn't hear my own thoughts—only the verses, the relentless verses, demanding more, always more. When Moros found me in the translator's study I was afraid I'd write myself into oblivion, he didn't tell me to suffer for my art—he sat beside me in the candlelight and helped me find silence between the lines. He brewed me bitter teas, pressed cool cloths to my fevered skin, and told me, 'If only we had the elixir, child, the muses would not demand so much of you.'"

The Honorable Justice Themis:
Thank you to the brave students for testifying.
May your creativity flow ever effortlessly,
and never be a detriment to your health and your sanity.
Please bring forward the Expert Testimonies.

First Expert: ***The Graphoanalysis Expert***
"I examined the professor's handwriting in the calligrapher's tower over the past two years, and the shift is undeniable—his once meticulous script grew erratic, frantic, as though he were writing against time itself. His final entries before the theft tremble with desperation, the ink pressed so hard into the parchment it nearly tore, as if he believed fate itself could be rewritten if only his hand were steady enough."

Second Expert: ***The Cartomancer***
"I read his cards with the gazing ball tarot underground in the hall of the gods the night before he vanished and I saw skyscrapers burning, bats hanging from the ceiling, and an omen of a poisoned weapon. The Tower, the Hanged Man, the Ten of Swords—ruin, sacrifice, and a pain too great to bear alone. He did not steal out of greed but out of fear, hoping to shift the cosmic design before another artist's candle flickered out too soon."

Third Expert: ***The Oracle Seer***
"The stars whispered his sorrow before he ever spoke it aloud—

I saw him standing at the loom of fate, tethered to the golden thread of the elixir, trembling as the Fates turned their hollow eyes upon him as he lost control. His crime was not hubris, but love, for he sought to mend in these students what even the gods had let unravel."

The Honorable Justice Themis:
Thank you to wonderful experts for your testimony.
Please bring forward the Divine Patrons for their statements.

Statement One: **Nyx, Goddess of Night**
"In the shadows where mortal minds break, I watched him linger—his dreams were restless, tangled with the echoes of suffering artists who had fallen before him. He did not steal in malice, but in grief, hoping to carve a path through the darkness before another soul was lost to it."

Statement Two: **Apollo, God of Music**
"I have seen countless artists kneel at my altar, begging for brilliance, for vision, for just one more masterpiece before they shatter under its weight—Moros saw what I refused to, that inspiration can become a curse. He sought not to defy me, but to undo the cruelty of the gift I so freely bestow."

Statement Three: **Clotho, Spinner of Fate**
"I felt his hands tremble upon the loom, pulling at threads not his to touch, but his heart was not driven by greed—it was raw, aching, desperate to stop the pattern of suffering that has woven for centuries. He thought himself the mender of fate, but even I do not know if such a thing is capable."

Statement Four: **Aphrodite, Goddess of Love**
"I have seen love in many forms—fierce, gentle, fleeting, eternal—but the love Moros holds for his students is unlike any I have witnessed. It is not the love of a teacher or a mentor, but of a protector, one who would bear the burden of their pain to shield them from the darkness that threatens to consume their spirits. Such devotion deserves more than punishment; it deserves a chance for renewal. I recommend the restoration of his mind and the healing of himself that has cracked beneath the weight of his own compassion."

The Honorable Justice Themis:
Thank you Divine Patrons, may your power be an inspiration to all of the students who reside here at the Academy.
Please bring forward the closing statements.

Closing statements by
The Prosecution team of Mount Olympus:

"Professor Moros may have acted out of misguided love, but his theft disrupted the delicate balance of creation itself, threatening to unravel the very fabric of artistic inspiration. No matter his intentions, the law must hold, for without consequences, there is no order—and without order, the muses will fade into silence."

Closing Statements by
The Defense team for Professor Moros:

"Professor Moros' actions, though unlawful, were driven by a deep and unyielding desire to save those who suffer under the weight of their own brilliance. He sought not to defy the gods, but to heal the very brokenness they have allowed to flourish— and for this, he deserves not punishment, but compassion and the chance to restore what has been lost."

Verdict as presented by the Honorable Judge Themis:
"While the law must stand firm, we must also recognize the depth of love and sacrifice that guided Professor Moros' actions—his desire to heal, rather than harm, cannot be ignored. Out of love, we shall bend the law to give him a chance to restore and mend his fractured mind, committing him to the healing pools of the Water Nymphs' Glade. However, his actions will not go without consequence—he shall no longer be allowed to teach or guide others, for even the brightest creators must learn that their gifts come with great responsibility. But I do recommend that he continue his pursuit of creativity and continue to tell his tale to the end of days or whence it becomes legend. Because creativity and art is something that should never be foregone and will always heal."

chapter 3:
the academy installs sonnets

on three brass plaques
across the institution
to preserve the history

—

The Elixir's Temptation
    Euterpe's First Sonnet
        plaque installed
        in the Letterpress Lab

In shadowed halls where muses weep,
Professor Moros sought a mystic brew,
The Elixir of Euterpe's secrets hidden deep,
And his quest for power in darkened view.

Through ancient tomes and forbidden paths tread,
To find a potion that could wield the gods,
A brew to crown him, the darkened shadows were fed,
His ambition danced and the darkness nods.

Yet in the corridors of artistry,
The students sensed the threat of looming night,
Divine intervention became a symphony,
As gods and pupils joined a judicial fight.

Euterpe's elixir and a sirens' call,
Became shadows encroaching, as students stood against it all.

Divine Justice Against The Theft
        Euterpe's Second Sonnet
            plaque installed
        at the entrance to the Library
            in the Poet's Courtyard.

Guided by visions, the students arose,
A trio gifted within the gods' embrace,
Judge Themis' wisdom with strategy flows,
And Aphrodite's love lending divine grace.

With verses spun the seer spoke,
Of prophecies and shadows becoming intertwined,
The story's brush was a canvas to invoke,
and thus the truth became aligned.

Apollo with music wove sonic strands,
A melody entwined with divine might,
In chorus gods and students took their stands,
To redeem Moros' quest and to send shadows taking flight.

In unity, they faced the scales of justice near,
Honest intention was in this case a motive clear.

Justice Restores Honest Artistry
    Euterpe's Third Sonnet
     plaque installed
     in the Sanctum of the Muses

In the Academy depths, a courtroom should convene,
Where Moros' actions faced Judge Themis' gaze,
The students, witnesses to what they had seen,
A tale of misguided hope and passion ablaze.

The Judge saw with eyes of love's grace
Yet warned of the malicious danger that Moros sought,
Still throughout a divine love in this sacred place,
Became a safeguard for the artistry he fought.

Rehabilitation, the verdict echoed through the hall,
A deed so dangerous and such a reckless quest,
Yet in this tale, a lesson to recall,
The balance of creativity carries a sweet bequest.

The imbalance now banished,
the students and gods stand,
Preserving creativity once again
with a united hand.

BIOS

DEE ALLEN
African-Italian performance poet based in Oakland, California. Active in creative writing & Spoken Word since the early 1990s. Author of 10 books--*Boneyard, Unwritten Law, Stormwater, Skeletal Black, Elohi Unitsi, Rusty Gallows: Passages Against Hate, Plans, Crimson Stain, Discovery* and his newest, *The Mansion*--and 78 anthology appearances under his figurative belt so far.

SUSAN P. BLEVINS
Susan P. Blevins, an ex-pat Brit, lived in Italy for twenty-six years, traveled the world extensively, and has now settled in Houston, Texas, where she is enjoying writing stories and poems based on her travels and adventures. She had a weekly column on food in a European newspaper while living in Rome, and has published various articles on gardens and gardening while living in northern New Mexico, before moving to Houston. Since living in Houston she has been published in various literary magazines, both in hard copy and online. her passions are classical music, gardening, nature, animals (cats in particular), reading and of course, writing. She has written a journal since she was about nine. She is a true bibliophile and has books in every room of her house.

ROGER CAMP
Roger Camp is the author of three photography books including the award winning Butterflies in Flight, Thames & Hudson, 2002. His documentary photography has been awarded the prestigious Leica Medal of Excellence. His work has appeared in numerous journals including *The New England Review, North American Review* and the *New York Quarterly*. Represented by the Robin Rice Gallery, NYC, more of his work may be seen on Luminous-Lint.com.

MICKEY COLLINS
Mickey ~~rights wrongs~~. Mickey ~~wrongs rites~~. Mickey writes words, sometimes wrong words but he tries to get it write.

LAVINIA DARR
Lavinia Darr is the pen name of a queer, disabled, feminist-horror author. She works in journal production at a small academic press specializing in mathematics, alongside her cat who would much prefer she put down the

laptop and instead figure out how to break open her rib cage so he may crawl inside.

Sarah Das Gupta
Sarah Das Gupta is a retired English teacher from near Cambridge, UK. She taught in India, Tanzania as well as the UK. As the head of department, she was often charged with overseeing the English section of the School Library and purchasing books.In most schools she was also responsible for stocking class libraries. She started writing this year after an accident which kept her in hospital. Her work has been published in many magazines from twelve countries, including US, UK, Australia, Canada, India, Germany, Croatia and Romania. Writing has given her the challenge and drive to learn to walk again.

Lores Denison
Lores Denison wrote her first book about a family of kittens when she was 8 years old. Since then she has been published in *Pensworth* and *Deep Overstock* literary journals. When she's not writing in a cafe, she can usually be found traipsing about the woods somewhere.

Lynette Esposito
Lynette G. Esposito, MA Rutgers, has been published in *Poetry Quarterly*, *North of Oxford*, *Twin Decades*, *Remembered Arts*, *Reader's Digest*, *US1*, and others. She was married to Attilio Esposito and lives with eight rescued muses in Southern New Jersey.

Robert Eversmann
Robert Eversmann works for *Deep Overstock*.

Kate Falvey
Kate Falvey's work has been published in many journals (including previous issues of *DO*) and anthologies; in a full-length collection, *The Language of Little Girls* (David Robert Books); and in two chapbooks, *What the Sea Washes Up* (Dancing Girl Press) and *Morning Constitutional in Sunhat and Bolero* (Green Fuse Poetic Arts). She co-founded (with Monique Ferrell) and for ten years edited the *2 Bridges Review*, published through City Tech (City University of New York) where she teaches, and is an associate editor for the *Bellevue Literary Review*.

John Grey
John Grey is an Australian poet, US resident, recently published in New World Writing, North Dakota Quarterly and Lost Pilots. Latest books, "Between Two Fires", "Covert" and "Memory Outside The Head" are

available through Amazon. Work upcoming in California Quarterly, Birmingham Arts Journal, La Presa and Soul Ink. I have spent a lifetime as a curator of my own library which has historically contained more books than I will ever hope to read.

HEATHER HAMBLEY

Heather is a Latin teacher turned translator. She has a BA in Classics from Reed College, where she developed a passion for prose composition and mythological women. She lives in Central Oregon with her husband Andy and their senior poodle Mo. She loves watching scary movies and curates feel-good horror sets at happyspookies.substack.com.

VALERIE HUNTER

Valerie Hunter worked at her college library as an undergrad, where she occasionally read the new acquisitions when she should have been shelving. She now teaches high school English and maintains a classroom library with a sadly low circulation rate. Her poems have appeared in publications including *Room Magazine, Wizards in Space,* and *Frost Meadow Review.*

RJ EQUALITY INGRAM

RJ Equality Ingram works as a used bookseller for Goodwill Industries of the Collumbia Willamette. Their first collection of poetry *The Autobiography of Nancy Drew* is forthcoming from White Stag Publishing in early 2024. RJ received their MFA in creative writing from Saint Mary's College of California with concentrations in poetry & creative nonfiction. More work can be found in *Phoebe Journal, Miniskirt Magazine* & *Citron Review* among others. RJ's cat Brenda lost a leg designing her memory palace.

ALETHA IRBY

Aletha Irby is very grateful to have been granted this time, on this planet, to spend with the English language. Her personal library includes books of poetry, books about cats (fiction and nonfiction), history books, novels, short story collections, mysteries, horror stories, classics, and books on calligraphy since as well as being a poet she is a calligrapher.

MONA MEHAS

Mona Mehas (she/her) writes poetry and prose from the perspective of a retired disabled teacher in Indiana USA. A Pushcart Prize nominee, her work has appeared in over 70 journals, anthologies, and online museums including Paddler Press Trip Log and IHRAM Literary magazine. Her poetry chapbooks, *Questions I Didn't Know I'd Asked* and *Hand-Me-Downs* are available on Amazon. Two of Mona's poems received first place honors in the 2023 Poetry Society of Indiana Fall contest. Mona is Editor-in-Chief of

Cicada Song Press and 2nd VP for Poetry Society of Indiana. She is searching for a home for her first novel and working on a novel in verse.

James B. Nicola

James B. Nicola is a returning contributor. The latest three of his eight full-length poetry collections are *Fires of Heaven: Poems of Faith and Sense*, *Turns & Twists*, and *Natural Tendencies*. His nonfiction book *Playing the Audience* won a Choice magazine award. A graduate of Yale, James has received a Dana Literary Award, two Willow Review awards, Storyteller's People's Choice magazine award, one Best of Net, one Rhysling, and eleven Pushcart nominations—for which he feels both stunned and grateful.

Timothy Arliss OBrien

Timothy Arliss OBrien (he/they) is an interdisciplinary artist in music composition, writing, and visual art. He has premiered music from opera to film scores to electronic ambient projects. He has published several books of poetry, (*The Queer Revolt*, *The Art of Learning to Fly*, & *Happy LGBTQ Wrath Month*), and is a poetry editor for *Deep Overstock*, a judge for Reedsy Prompts, and a poetry reader for *Okay Donkey*. He also founded the podcast & small press publishing house, The Poet Heroic, and the digital magic space The Healers Coven. He also showcases his psychedelic makeup skills as the phenomenal drag queen Tabitha Acidz.
Check out more at his website: www.timothyarlissobrien.com

Colm O'Shea

I have worked as a bookseller at Barnes & Noble in NYC, and a librarian in Cork Central Library, Ireland. I'm currently a writing teacher at New York University, but I work in conjunction with the Bobst librarians to teach students research skills, and to occasionally lead them into the Narnian wonderland that is the stacks.

Olivia Park

Olivia Park is a high school student who loves storytelling. She enjoys writing poetry, short stories, and essays that explore themes of identity and the human experience. Olivia has been recognized in school literary magazines and local competitions. When not writing, she finds inspiration in art, music, and nature.

bart plantenga

bart plantenga is the author of novels Beer Mystic, Radio Activity Kills, & Ocean GroOve, short story collection Wiggling Wishbone, novella Spermatagonia: The Isle of Man & wander memoirs: Paris Scratch & NY Sin Phoney in Face Flat Minor. He's one of the founding members of the NYC agit-prankster-writer group, The Unbearables. His books YODEL-AY-EE-OOOO: The Secret History of Yodeling Around the World & Yodel in HiFi & the CD Rough Guide to Yodel have created the misunderstanding that he's the world's foremost yodel expert. He produces 2 monthly podcasts: Dig•Scape & iMMERSE!. He's also a DJ & has produced Wreck This Mess in NYC, Paris, Amsterdam, Rotterdam since forever. He lives in Amsterdam.

Susan L. Pollet
Susan L. Pollet is a visual artist whose works have appeared in multiple art shows and literary publications. She studied at the New York Art Students League, has been a member since 2018, and resides in NYC. She is also a published author in multiple genres, including three children's books, which she both wrote and illustrated. She has seen the darker sides of humanity, but always searches for the light.

Justin Ratcliff
Justin Ratcliff is a new emerging poet, who was cast into the depths of himself during the Covid-19 outbreak. Born, raised, and still preceding in South Central Alaska. From a very early age he had found a haven in his local library. Each new book was a new world in which to escape the harsh realities of life's bitter brew. Draws much of his inspirations from psychology, philosophy, theology, nature, and dark fantasy.

Abigail Ray
Abigail Ray is a writer from Portland, Oregon and has been published in Same Faces Collective, Maudlin House, and Call Me Brackets. She recently graduated with her Bachelor's in English and writing and is looking forward to a lucrative career path of Gay Barista™ She loves writing poetry and experimental fiction about loser-core women that are definitely not poorly disguised projections of herself, no matter what people are saying.

Jihye Shin
Jihye Shin is a Korean-American poet and bookseller based in Florida.

Al Simon, Jr.
I am a veteran who was born and raised in Des Moines, Iowa. I have self-published The People Downstairs Are Killers, have published a short story with Men Matters Online Journal and have an upcoming nonfiction piece to be published by Wilderness Literary Journal in April. I also have several works at Smashwords.

Dana Wall
I found this document wedged between Borges and Bradbury, its pages still warm, leaking what might be ink or consciousness. As someone who spent twenty years as a CPA before pursuing an MFA at Goddard College, I recognize the signs of a system evolving beyond its original purpose.

Nicholas Yandell
Nicholas Yandell is a composer, who sometimes creates with words instead of sound. In those cases, he usually ends up with fiction and occasionally poetry. He also paints and draws, and often all these activities become combined, because they're really not all that different from each other, and it's all just art right?
When not working on creative projects, Nick works as a bookseller at Powell's Books in Portland, Oregon, where he enjoys being surrounded by a wealth of knowledge, as well as working and interacting with creatively stimulating people. He has a website where he displays his creations; it's nicholasyandell.com. Check it out!

Alexis Blaire Zielke
Alexis Blaire Zielke paints, writes and does 1:1 sessions with people, listening and talking about non-duality. She published her first book, The Nothing, on Halloween of 2024. The book is inspired by the antagonist of the Film, The NeverEnding Story, and is illustrated with drawings of endangered animals. The book is available on Kickstarter.com.
The Mental Landscapes series is a practice of painting from memory. A practice where anything can arise. A practice without awareness as to what is arising. Anything is allowed. Surprise, surprise, surprise... And so, a tulip is not a tulip, but a memory of many tulips, and peonies, and dahlias combined into a unique, imaginary plant. A person is not exactly someone I have met before, but many faces, many feelings, and many expressions. Experience translates into impressions. Impressions are expressed in color and form.